7/93

HAYWIRE

HAYWIRE

Jim Caplette

HARBOUR PUBLISHING

Published by
HARBOUR PUBLISHING
P.O. Box 219
Madeira Park, BC Canada V0N 2H0

Edited by Tom Henry
Cover design by Roger Handling
Cover illustration by Greta Guzek
Printed and bound in Canada

Canadian Cataloguing in Publication Data

Caplette, Jim, 1924--

Haywire

Originally published under title: Gopher tales.
ISBN 1-55017-084-8
1. Caplette, Jim, 1924--   2. Canadian wit and humor
(English).*   I. Title. II. Title: Gopher tales.
PS8555.A64H3 1993   C818'.5402   C93-091513-5
PR9199.3.C36H3 1993

Many, many thanks to my longtime friend David French for all
his yeoman work in attempting to create some semblance of
form and order out of all this chaos.

                                                              J.C.

For my mother, Ursula (Ushi), who came from Switzerland and turned a prairie life of unimaginable poverty into a triumph of happiness and love.

CONTENTS

Foreword   *David French*   9

I. Living in Lotus Land

Bear Country   15
Hangin' the E Plate   18
Lamp Black and Used Car Oil   21
Ripple Rock   28
Postal Department   33
Leon's Little Pet   35
Piles, Purgatory and Hell   37
The Pinto's Last Rites   40
Shortcut to the Teahouse   45
Pet Rock, Skookum Size   49
Fishing with Tony   51
Band-Aids Under the Bridge   57
The Parts Department   61

II. Growing Up on the Prairies

Schtoopid Kids   71
Louis Caplette   75
The City Kid Hitches a Tow   78
We're Going to Delmas   80
The Great Gopher War   85
Joe's Cafe   89
Old Wives' Tales   92
My Aunt Pat   96
Poison Shmoizen   98
With This Ring   100
Go for the Horses   102
A Hot Beef Sandwich   106
Tapping Maples   108
The Mortgage Company   110

III. Cariboo / Interior / Okanagan

Church Parade	123
Towing George's Logging Truck	125
Cariboo Picnic	129
Rassling a Grizzly	133
One for the Road in Williams Lake	137
The Last Great White Hunter	140
Taming the Similkameen	144

IV. Pots Pureed

What's in a Name?	151
Ape-olution	153
This Old House—A Horror Story	157
Have You Got a Pocketknife?	159
Sleep Walkin'	161
Cashing It In	163
Lying and Dying	165
The Wood Stove	167
Recycling	168
Talkin' to Myself	170
Kin Ya Card A Gitar, Bye?	172
I Want to Look at the Trees	174
The Word	177

V. Some Folks I've Known

My Buddy Al Brown	183
Gary the Fiddle Man	189
Canada Geese—and Candidly Royal	192
Betty's Birthday Bash	198
Mexican Train Wreck	200
Brown Beats BC Hydro?	208
Wanna Buy a Duck?	212
The Brick	215
Windows in the Dark	218
Happiness	223

Foreword

The first time I dropped by Jim's house, he was walking up and down his lawn, pushing a strange contraption that resembled a lawn mower. It was almost soundless.

"That's the quietest lawn mower I've ever heard," I remarked. "Who makes it?"

His reply was as autobiographical as it was descriptive.

"Well, the mower body and the wheels I found in the old North Van dump, but the gasoline engine was shot so I threw it away—can't stand those noisy, smokin' bloody things anyway."

"What about the electric motor sitting on top," I asked, "did you get that at the dump too?"

"Yep," he answered. "I just bolted that electric motor on top and hooked it directly to the blade underneath."

"Does it work okay?"

"Can't rightly say," he replied, "I've only been running it for nineteen years. But so far, so good."

I couldn't help noticing that Jim was wearing an ancient-looking pair of open-toed wooden clogs, so I commented, "I suppose you got those clogs from the dump too."

"Nope. A friend of mine bought a house from a Danish

fellow about twenty-five years ago, and that crazy Dane had thrown these clogs into his trash can. I recapped them with soles I cut from an old tire and I replaced the leather top on one of them, but the wooden parts were as good as new. Them new soles have been on there now for twelve years."

Later, as we walked through Jim's back yard, I noticed his garage was covered with shake siding.

"Did you build your own garage?" I asked.

"Yep," said Jim. "I cut them shakes myself about forty years ago. Good, thick, hand-split barn shakes like that should last a hundred years."

In keeping with someone who has many projects on the go at a time, Jim's workshop and his outside sheds make Fibber McGee's hall closet look neat and tidy. I asked if he had plans for all the junk.

"Junk is what other people collect," he replied. "This is all good stuff."

It soon became obvious that Jim was a natural-born recycler, a do-it-yourselfer, a tinkerer and a pack rat, all rolled into one.

Jim was born in 1924, on a dairy farm three miles south of Battleford, Saskatchewan. He attended the St. Vital separate school up to grade eight, and many a time during lunch break he would hike to the abandoned police barracks south of the school. Of all those old weatherbeaten buildings, Jim's favourite was the ancient jail, where his great-grandfather Charlie Bremner was once imprisoned in a cell next to Louis Riel.

Jim attended Battleford Collegiate till halfway through grade ten when, at the age of sixteen, he headed for Vancouver. Just as his favourite teacher Mr. Mkeechuck had done, Jim got a job in the Burrard Shipyards and started making some "real money."

After a short stint in the army, Jim took a course in auto mechanics and worked for several large auto dealerships in the Vancouver area. Then, for twenty years, he ran his own small trucking business in North Vancouver.

In 1990, Jim sort of retired. I say "sort of" because he now works twice as hard as ever and spends a lot of time helping his friend Al Brown work on a fishing boat that's being donated to the poverty-stricken fishermen in Nicaragua. His hobbies include working with red or yellow cedar and with driftwood, which he transforms into strange and wonderful *objets d'art*.

Music has always been Jim's first love, and he still sings and plays trumpet, guitar, and tub bass every week or two in hotels and pubs with his buddy Gary Comeau, a professional musician.

He tells me his other passions are writing, politics and bullshitting, not necessarily in that order. Philosophically speaking, Jim only gives two pieces of advice: Don't walk on green logs, and don't step on the ants.

Although strangers may at first mistake his individuality for eccentricity, Jim has both feet planted firmly in the soil. In fact, he mentioned one time that his epitaph should read, "He still had some shakes to cut."

DAVID FRENCH

I.

Living in Lotus Land

Bear Country

Wistful Vista was the name of a cedar cabin on the banks of the Seymour River. It was two miles up Pipeline Road, beside which ran a huge water main that carried water to the City of Vancouver, and the last residence before the Greater Vancouver Water Board's NO TRESPASSING sign. The cabin was completely surrounded by towering firs and cedars that clung to the stone canyon walls of the river.

Except for the roar of the river below, and the odd noisy raven, it was a regular hideaway paradise. Kids would scramble down the cliffs in summer and dive twenty or thirty feet off the rocks into deep pools of that crystal clear, super-cold mountain water. They emerged to lie steaming on the immense sunbaked boulders that stayed warm from noon to sundown. To someone like myself, who came from burnt-out Saskatchewan, the green ferns and salmonberries looked like salad.

Salmonberries, my sister Ruth told me one afternoon soon after I arrived, are the favourite food of black bears. She and her husband Harry were renting Wistful Vista, and I was staying with them till I could find a room of my own closer to the shipyard where I was working. To a kid fresh off the prairies, mere mention of the word "bears" was enough to conjure visions of carnivorous man-eating monsters.

"Bears?" I said. "You mean there are bears around?"

"Sure," she said matter-of-factly.

"You mean right around here?"

"Sure, Skippy chases them nearly every night." Skippy was a small fox terrier Ruth and Harry had brought out when they moved from Saskatoon a year or so before.

There it was, a bloody plague in paradise: bears. I started thinking I'd better get the hell out of there, and the sooner the better.

Now some people would say Ruth had a perverted sense of humour. I think "diabolical" would be a more fitting description. Who else would tell her younger brother to lick that sparkling doorknob on a forty-below Saskatchewan morning? Yep, my favourite sister.

There was no fridge in the cabin, so milk, eggs and butter were kept in a screened cooler out in the carport. That evening Harry asked me casually if I'd go out and get some milk from the cooler. I didn't know it, but Ruth had snuck out and crawled under their Model A Ford in the carport. I was barefoot, and as I picked my way gingerly over the gravel I was all ears and eyes for bears. I grabbed the milk and was alongside the Model A when something grabbed my leg. The milk went flying. I took off like a cheetah for a quarter mile down the road, not giving a damn for those sharp rocks on my bare feet. Ruth crawled out, hysterical with laughter. The city was looking better all the time.

Because the cabin was so small, I had to sleep in a hammock on the verandah, facing the river.

"What about bears?" I asked.

"Skippy can sleep with you," Ruth replied. "He'll bark if any bears come around."

Back home, the biggest wild animals (if you didn't count the threshing crews on payday) were gophers. I was wondering, what in hell am I doing out here in the jungles of BC? Well, I laid in that hammock two or three hours, staring into the trees and listening, the dog sleeping on my feet.

Suddenly, out of the black, I heard something like claws scratching on wood, then more scratching, and coming up those verandah steps was a huge black bear's head, mouth wide open. I was damn lucky the evening was warm and the cabin doors were ajar. That way, when I went flying through, nothing got broken, including me. Harry hollered, "What in hell's going on?" as I crashed in the back door, out the front door and down the same damn road I'd escaped on earlier. Soon I heard him shouting, "It's okay, the bear's gone."

When I walked back in, Ruth was laughing so hard she couldn't speak. Harry was giving her hell for playing such a stupid trick. She had taken a bearskin—the kind with head, claws, fangs and all—out of their bedroom, put it on her back, and clawed and scratched her way up the back steps. Harry was afraid I might have picked up a chair and clubbed that bear over the head, thereby giving Ruth a headache. I could have told him his fears were groundless. When it comes to me and bears, and the fight or flight response, I'll take the latter, thank you very much. Next day, I found a room in town. The bears I could handle, but my sister Ruth, she was just too damn much.

Sometimes in the evening when things are just a little too serene, I wish she were still alive to scare the hell out of me one more time.

Hangin' the E Plate

The ten-thousand-ton Victory class ship, of the kind built by
Burrard Dry Dock in North Vancouver during the Second
World War, was a helluva tough ship. It wasn't torpedo-proof
mind you, but you never heard of Victory class freighters breaking apart in a rough sea like the American-built, Liberty class,
all-welded "Kaiser jobs" often did. Victory ships, unlike the
American types, were riveted and welded only at the points
where the enormous plates that formed the hull butted together.
This increased the hull's flexibility and lessened metal fatigue.

As a kid of sixteen I was hired by Burrard as a plate hanger.
Assembling a Victory ship in those days was like putting together
a giant jigsaw—the plates were lettered A--J and marked PORT or
STAR for starboard. These plates were placed against the frame
of the ship, and our job was to secure them with bolts. Behind
us came the bolting-up crews, reaming crews, riveting crews
and, finally, the welders, caulkers and painters. This was all done
in a hell of a hurry, as the Germans were sinking our ships as
fast as we were making them. Burrard held the record for
building a ship: from start to launching, thirty-nine days.

Building steel-hulled riveted ships must have been a boon

to the hearing aid business, because it was the noisiest damn place I ever worked in. The whine of the overhead cranes and welding machines, the scream of the air-powered reamers, the constant sledge-hammering of the fitters, the high-pitched rap of the caulking guns, the constant starting and stopping of air compressors, the screech of the huge riveting and bucking up guns—what a hell of a symphony those tools produced! Most communication had to be done by hand signals if you were more than two or three feet away, and even at that distance you had to holler to get above the noise.

The plate hangers (who were later to be named "erector specialists," if you please) worked in gangs of five—four workers and a charge hand. The charge hand was somebody with a loud voice who preferably knew that port was not exclusively a European wine, and starboard meant right. A couple of weeks experience in shipbuilding helped, as did knowledge of some basic hand signals for the huge overhead cranes. Proper crane signals were critical when working below those heavy plates, before the first few bolts held them fast.

The charge hand on my crew was a big redhead who wanted to set the world record for hanging plates, and maybe get some brownie points in the bargain. At least that's how it appeared to us. Plate hanging was dangerous at the best of times, but whenever someone tried to move a lot of heavy objects too fast, it was just plain stupid. That didn't bother Red, even though the ambulance was in that yard two, maybe three times a day. And a lot of those times, the driver didn't have to hurry on his way back to the hospital.

I, for one, was too young to find out if there really was a hereafter. I also figured if we didn't build those ships so fast, the Germans couldn't sink 'em so fast. But old Red—he must have been thirty—he just kept rushing around.

Now the most difficult part of the job was hanging the E plate. The plates were listed alphabetically from the keel, and the E plate was at the point where the bottom curled up the side. In other words, it was the first vertical plate in the water.

This plate was left till the last to give workers access to the inside of the hull. The problem was that while all the other plates were lapped about six inches over the plates immediately below, the E plate had to be tucked inside of the D plate below, as well as the F plate above. This was a real tricky operation and required a lot of plain bull-work and patience. That plate was such a mean mother it should have been called the F plate. Come to think of it, most of the time it was called that "effen plate."

The configuration of the hull at the aft, near the propellor shaft, meant the plate had to be lowered roughly to the right level by the crane, then pulled in toward the keel with block and tackle. The crane would slack the cables and we would pinch bar the plate down and past where it belonged to get under the plate above, then go up with the crane to pull the plate into place.

This one day, Red was in his usual panic. As the crane lowered the E plate, we kept manoeuvring it to clear the scaffolding beside the hull. We managed to pull the plate in and get the bottom edge hooked under the lower plate. Then old Red signalled a relay man, who in turn signalled the crane operator, to let down more slack. We got slack all right—hell, there must have been two feet of loose cable. No way could that plate stay pinched in. Luckily I stepped clear just as the plate let go and swung out a good fifteen feet, knocking Red and two of the crew off the scaffold into the water. For a few seconds there were just three hard hats floating. Then up bobbed three heads spitting out that scummy water. The hardest work I did that day was trying not to laugh out loud, I was killing myself inside. Seeing old Red dog-paddling to shore was a sight for sore eyes.

"You guys were lucky the tide was in, otherwise you could have got hurt," I said.

Old Red suggested I go fuck off. Then all three headed for home with the water sloshing out of their boots. I went home, too—I had to, my guts were just too sore from laughing.

Red slowed down a little after that, especially hangin' the E plate.

Lamp Black and Used Car Oil

Does anyone remember when you could buy ten acres of good, high, dry ground for one thousand dollars? And I'm talking about ten acres with a three-room house, a barn, a chicken coop, a well, an outhouse, a three-acre hay field and a winding driveway with huge fir and cedar trees. No, it wasn't in the last century. It wasn't even during the depression. It was in the late forties, and I was the guy that bought that farm.

Why, you ask, would a guy working as a mechanic in Vancouver buy acreage thirty miles away, near White Rock? Well, it was like this: My brother-in-law and my sister Betty, who was a registered nurse, purchased a lodge near Cloverdale that had been converted to an old-age home. The space that had been set aside for management and staff proved to be much too cramped for them to live in, so when my sister spied this acreage for sale in the Cloverdale paper, she phoned her "rich brother"— me.

Betty went on about how nice the place was and the advantages of living in the clean, quiet, peaceful countryside, what a great place it would be to raise kids, and how it would be a good investment in case Vancouver grew larger. The property also happened to be a stone's throw away from my sister's lodge (provided, that is, you could throw a stone like that little guy in the Bible who nailed the big guy between the eyes with his sling).

There were just a few minor problems in paradise my sister failed to mention. To start with, the bumpy old Pacific Highway that led to White Rock sat on top of a peat bog and went up and down like a roller coaster, depending on the tides from Mud Bay. I would have to travel this goat trail twice a day from my job at Begg Motor Company in Vancouver. Nor did she mention the nightmare of navigating the Pattullo Bridge, an exercise only slightly less hazardous than playing Russian roulette the hard way, with one chamber left empty. In fact, there were many things she forgot to mention, like trees over power lines and no water in the summertime. But what the hell, that's what sisters are for, right?

Now it just happened that this was the one and only time in my life so far that I had ever found myself possessed of so much as two hundred dollars cash, so I signed the deal. My wife Grace and I piled our possessions onto a utility trailer, hitched it to my four-door '41 Plymouth sedan, and off we went.

Our new house was small, but it was a hell of a lot bigger than the single room with hot plate in east Vancouver where we had spent the last three years. It was also quiet—a bit like what the nuns told me heaven must be like—except, of course, for frogs, crickets and birds. And the air: it smelled of timothy, mint and cedar, especially when it rained.

"I'll check the well," I said, shortly after we unloaded the furniture. Lifting the weathered planks, I was astounded by the mass of spider webs strung across the top. It was a bright day, and trying to see the water twenty feet down was quite difficult. Soon, I spied something moving in the water. It was a garter snake. Also floating there were another snake and a mole, but they had gone to their reward. One more thing my sister never mentioned.

I know garter snakes are good swimmers, but nothing

swims forever. So I got a bucket, put some weight on one side to make it tip over when it hit the water, tied on about thirty feet of rope, and lowered it gently down the well. On my first attempt, too much water got inside the bucket before I manoeuvred it under the snake, and he swam right out. Snakes may be pretty, but they ain't too bright. Next, I tried a half-bucket of water and I had a snake. I carried him into the hay field and asked him if he would mind playing in the neighbours' well for a change. He took off with not even a backward glance. That's gratitude for ya.

One more cast with the bucket and I retrieved the snake's dead brother. He must have been down there a long time, his colours had mostly faded. I know snakes are beneficial animals and through the centuries they have suffered a bad press, but still and all, I don't fancy them flavouring my drinking water.

That left me with the dead mole. I dropped the bucket and accidentally hit him square. When I lifted the bucket, that mole had completely disintegrated and was slowly covering the whole top of the well. So much for country living.

I now had no choice but to hire a pump, pump the well dry and build a concrete crib with a tight top so all them damn critters couldn't commit suicide.

One other thing the country has that you don't find in the city is neighbours. Yep, whether you need them or not, you got neighbours. So I'm sitting on the well, putting little pins in a doll that was the likeness of my sister, when I hear a loud, "Hello, hello." This wizened old guy had a decibel reading roughly that of the Point Atkinson Lighthouse foghorn.

I was about to remark, "Look mister, stupidity is my problem, not a loss of hearing." I later learned his hearing was nearly gone, along with most of his stomach, his eyesight, one knee and various other parts.

"I'm Jack Webster," he said, sticking out a hand. "This used to be Johnny Hardbottle's place. That well needs some cribbing and a new top. Bleedin' thing should have been fixed years ago. I live next place over."

"Howdy," I said, and we shook hands.

He said, "You're gonna need tongue-and-groove cedar two-by-sixes for the top deck, it takes the weather better than fir." I told him about the snakes, and he said, "Johnny had the odd snake too. They won't kill ya." I'm thinkin' maybe they wouldn't kill Johnny, but I'm from the big city where we prefer our water neat.

"What about concrete?" I asked.

"First, we got to dig down to the hardpan," he said. "Then we need some shiplap and two-by-fours. Never mind, I got some back of the shed. You go and get three, no, make that four sacks of Portland cement. We can screen enough gravel right off the driveway. Don't worry about the decking right now, we can get that after we pour the concrete. I got a mixer."

Yessiree, the country has neighbours. Old Jack rubbed a lot of people the wrong way with his direct nosy approach to things and he had few friends. But he meant well and was always willing to lend a hand, whether you asked for it or not. All the while, he was dying of stomach cancer. I often miss the cantankerous old bugger.

One day, when Jack dropped over, I said, "Is that firewood stacked by the chicken coop any good to burn? And how come it's cut so big and long?"

"Hell boy," Jack snorted. "That's not firewood, those are shake blocks."

"Shake blocks? What are they?"

"Hold on," he said, heading back over the fence to his place. He soon reappeared, carrying a small hand axe: "This is for trimmin' the edges," he explained. In his other hand, he carried a huge iron slab probably eighteen or twenty inches long, three inches wide, and a quarter-inch thick. It was tapered, and sharpened along the lower edge, and one end had been heated and curled into a tight loop through which a stout, two-foot stake had been inserted. He also brought a huge, crude, well-scarred wooden mallet. "That's my persuader," he said. "Now fetch me one of those blocks."

I started to pick one up, but he said it was too knotty, and pointed to another. I laid it beside him. "Now stand it on end," he ordered. With a few concise strokes of the hand axe, he trimmed off the rough edges. Next, he placed this contraption—which he said was called "a froe, and don't ask me why"—three-quarters of an inch from one edge of the block and gave it a couple of healthy whacks with the wooden mallet. Then, he placed his good knee against the block, pulled on the froe handle, and—thunk—a beautiful, clear shake split off. It was bloody magic, and the cedar aroma was intoxicating.

"That's what you call barn shakes," Jack explained. "No taper. If you want taper, like shingles, you just turn the block over after every shake. Here, you try it."

After a few tries, I was creating my own shakes. It was fantastic! From that time to the present, I have always owned a shake froe. Through the years, I have hand split shakes for several houses, sheds and barns. I still think it's magic. A good hand-split shaked roof should last a hundred years. What's even better, they don't cost a nickel if you scrounge the cedar off the beach or off clearing jobs.

I still have a dozen shake blocks in my backyard and have shown many friends how to split them. Cuttin' shakes doesn't make you much money, but it could save a few trips to the shrink, and you always have lots of kindling for the fireplace from the trimmings. Yes sir, Jack, I owe you one for my apprenticeship.

But back to our new place at White Rock:

Within a week or two, Jack and I finished the well—concrete, deck, and all. I opened a bottle of Canadian Club, and with just a touch of well water that was seeping back after we had pumped her dry, we sat on the new deck, and Jack told me about the times he spent as an airframe mechanic in the Royal English Flying Corps, during the First World War.

The city seemed a long way off. A couple more drinks, and I was thinkin', "this is the life." I should become a hippie, phone the boss, tell him to shove the job. But I didn't have a phone, and hippies weren't invented yet. After a while Jack staggered home, and things settled down for a few days.

Next week, he comes over the fence and hollers, "Them shingles on the house are startin' to curl."

"I'll buy some paint," I said.

"Paint's no good for shingles," he replied.

"So what do I use?"

"You got some motor oil?"

"Yep, I got a few cans in the shop."

He snorted. "Naw, used oil. You got any used oil?"

"Hell, I got lotsa used oil. What do I need used oil for?"

"You go to the hardware store in Cloverdale and get five pounds of lamp black, mix it with five gallons of old oil and you got enough to cover that roof."

"What in hell is lamp black?" I asked.

"You was born on the prairie, wasn't ya?"

"Well yes, but . . ."

"You didn't have no electric lights, did ya?"

"No, but . . ."

"What happened to them coal oil lamps when the wick got too high?"

"Well, they got black."

"That's right," says Jack, "so you just ask at the hardware."

Old Jack didn't leave much room for negotiation or consultation. At the hardware in town, I ran into my uncle Chris who had a farm outside Langley. "How's the new place?" he asked.

"Good," I said, "but the shingles are startin' to curl. I'm going to treat them with lamp black and car oil."

"I never heard of anybody using that," he said.

"Neither did I, but the neighbour said it works good and that it's the best shingle preservative there is. Cheap, too." Then I asked him what works good for walkin' on old, slippery shingles.

"No problem," he said. "Just pull a pair of wool socks clean over your boots and you won't slip and you won't get any slivers either." I thanked him and headed for home with the lamp black.

In the yard, I filled a five-gallon can with used oil, dumped in the lamp black, and stirred. Then I pulled a pair of old socks over my boots, put up the wooden ladder, and with five gallons of that goop and an old whitewash brush, I climbed up.

I almost made the peak of the roof when my uncle's ingenious invention failed. Down that roof I went. I hit the ladder, and it swung me over in a slow, graceful arc—like a reverse pole vault—over the yard. I can't recall whether I saw my life flashing before my eyes, but I do remember noticing that the bucket of goop was still with me. And for a millisecond, I remembered something in high school physics about all objects falling at the same rate.

The ground slammed up, and suddenly I was lying flat with five gallons of goop covering me totally, my hair, my ears, my eyes—I was one hell of a mess. It was a good thing Jack wasn't watching from his usual spot across the fence because, in his delicate condition, a sight like that could have killed him.

Hearing the crash and commotion, Grace came running out of the house. When she found out I wasn't dead, she started to laugh. I was so mad I could have killed her, but I wanted to get at my uncle first. Two or three baths later, and I was able to see a little humour in the situation. Just a little, though.

P.S. The pins in the doll didn't work—my sister is as healthy as a horse.

P.P.S. There are two pieces of wisdom I should like to pass along: 1) When your shingles start to curl, call the roofer. He's in the Yellow Pages. 2) Keep your wool socks inside your leather boots, where they belong and where the good Lord intended for them to be.

Ripple Rock

From 1956 to 1964, I ran a small Imperial Oil service station at an intersection near the Second Narrows Bridge, which spans Burrard Inlet, a couple of miles east of the city of North Vancouver. The garage had a tiny apartment on the second floor, where my wife and I lived.

Much to the consternation of Esso, I probably sold less gas than any other service station in Canada. I had two antiquated pumps, one for plain old Esso, which was regular gas, and one for Esso Extra, which was for the well-heeled and cost a couple of cents more. No fancy gas bar or emporium, no sir. However, I was probably the first one in the country to introduce self-service, mainly because that was the only way my customers could get gas. By the time I strolled back from the cafe a block away (where I would talk politics and drink bad coffee with Max, the owner), my customers would have either pumped their own gas and left the money on the counter, or just blown their horns a few times and taken off in a cloud of dust and flying gravel (only the fancy stations had pavement around the pumps in those days).

The way I saw it, if the customer left mad and never came

back, I would have fewer interruptions when I was either at the cafe or under a car. On that point, Imperial Oil and I never did see eye to eye. Thirty years later, when all the gas companies introduced self-serve, I should have sued for patent infringement.

My self-serve station may not have been too popular with Imperial Oil, but it sure as hell was unforgettable for lots of other folks, including plenty of Yankees. Here's why.

On April 5, 1958, two million seven hundred thousand pounds of TNT tore the top off an underwater mountain peak known as Ripple Rock. It was the largest non-atomic explosion in history and it made headlines around the world. The tip of Ripple Rock had sat just under the water in the middle of Seymour Narrows, a busy passage near Campbell River on Vancouver Island. Over the years, it had claimed dozens and dozens of ships, from sail to steam to diesel, and at least 114 lives.

To get rid of this hazard, a shaft was sunk from a nearby island, five hundred feet down and a half-mile out under the sea. A rail line was laid to carry the blasted rock out and high explosive back in. The project took three years and, in the end, was a total success, leaving at least fifty feet of water over what used to be Ripple Rock.

During that same period, rock and gravel were being draglined from Lynn Creek, which passed a few hundred yards from my service station. The material from the creek bottom was trucked past my garage to a crushing plant in the Dollarton area, a mile or two away. One day, one of these overloaded trucks turned the corner too fast, and a huge boulder fell off and landed not more than fifty feet from the station. The rock was as round as a marble and weighed at least two hundred pounds. ("Kilograms" was a strange word from a far-off land in those times.)

Although a rock that size in the road could have been good for business—I specialized in alignments—I figured I'd better get it off the road. Good thing that boulder was round, otherwise I would never have been able to budge it. It must have been rolling in that creek bottom ten thousand years. I rolled it beside the pump island, dug out some black paint, and painted on the side of the rock, "Piece of Ripple Rock fell at this site April 5, 1958."

Then I went back to work.

Lots of locals stopped to read the inscription, have a laugh, and leave. But tourists, they didn't always get the joke. Americans, especially, would stop for gas and ask if that piece of rock really fell right there. "Yep," I'd say, "fell right there beside the pumps." Then they would get the kids out of the car and show them this phenomenon. Sometimes they sat the youngsters on the rock, making sure their legs didn't obscure the inscription, and snap a half-dozen pictures. I would have to disappear into the shop—I didn't dare crack up during such a solemn ritual.

If I hadn't seen it with my own eyes, I wouldn't have believed it. I could understand that tourists might not know Seymour Narrows is a hundred miles from North Vancouver. But what I couldn't understand was why they didn't ask how a rock that had been blasted could be so round and smooth. That's what got me. No wonder they made a bad cowboy actor into a president.

One night when I was away from my apartment, Pete, a perennial prankster, and my nephew Bruce Bathgate, a fellow jazz lover, decided to "borrow" my rock. They rassled and rolled it up a plank into the trunk of Pete's car and took off. They got about three blocks up the highway when an RCMP patrol car pulled them over. The officer had spotted them leaving my deserted station and suspected a robbery. After searching the car, the cop asked if there was anything in the trunk. Pete said no. "Let's have a look," persisted the Mountie.

Pete opened the trunk and the cop spied the rock. Pete tried to explain that it was just being borrowed, but the officer didn't buy the line. "You can't go around stealing a guy's rocks," he said. Then he made them go back to the station and struggle the rock back to its original position.

"Now, let's see if you really know this fellow," said the Mountie as he knocked on the door. It was lucky for those two jokers we weren't home, as I am quite sure I would have told that cop, "I never seen these guys before in my life." A man doesn't get an opportunity like that very often.

Anyway, getting no response, the Mountie gave them a further lecture and sent them on their way.

A week passed, and Pete and Bruce decided to kidnap my rock again. This time the heist was clean. They transported the rock to North Vancouver and rolled it up a plank onto the seat of their friend Ed's car. Ed was a quiet, mild-mannered guy, who continually and without complaint bore the brunt of many of Pete's practical jokes. On leaving for work next morning, Ed was astounded to find that huge stone (which had completely collapsed his seat springs) in his car. He tried easing the rock out, but it got away on him, tore off the front of his running board and put a huge dish in his dad's new asphalt driveway.

Ed knew there was only one dirty rat that would do such a thing, so he formulated a plan of attack. He rolled the rock into his dad's workshop, where he fashioned a steel cage and welded it around the rock. Then, on Friday, at about eleven in the evening, Ed and Bruce loaded the caged rock into the car and headed across the Second Narrows Bridge.

Ed knew that Pete was paid on Fridays and that he and his friends usually spent the entire evening in a Vancouver east end beer parlour. They spied Pete's car in the hotel parking lot. As quick as they could, they unloaded the rock, ran a short chain through the rear spring shackle of Pete's car, looped the other end through the steel cage, snapped the ends shut with a big padlock and left for home.

Later, when the pub closed, Pete staggered out, jumped into his car and threw her in reverse. There was a grinding crunch. Thinking he had hit a concrete curb, he put the car in low, shot ahead a foot and came to a shuddering stop. By now, several amused spectators had gathered, so Pete decided to investigate. He found he was tethered to a caged rock.

Pete's inclination was to kill Ed, but first he had to get mobile. He walked over a mile to find a service station open at that hour and borrowed a hacksaw. Then, to the delight of his friends, he had to crawl under the car and cut off that lock.

Next morning, the rock was back at my service station. Pete had brought it home. That poor old rock looked awful scruffy and burned, so I dragged it out back and gave it a decent burial. It was like losing an old friend.

Postal Department

When I was running my "self-service" station, I owned a white-haired terrier named Cisco. Cisco lived for two purposes only: fighting dogs and chasing postmen.

Cisco must have been in a thousand dog fights and never won a single one, mainly because the dogs he picked on were usually three to four times his size. I never could figure how he failed to learn from experience. Maybe he chased too many parked cars, or maybe he read that crap somewhere about "it's not the size of the dog in the fight, it's the size of the fight in the dog." In retrospect, I should have sent him for karate lessons. Anyway, I did admire his persistence.

One day I was working under a car when a postman walked by. Cisco spotted him, dashed out and bit him on the leg. This wasn't a nip—it was a real hard bite just above the ankle. It happened so fast I didn't even have time to holler. I felt bad for the postman, who was also a friend, and I told him that was Cisco's last bite. I said the old dog was going to go to that great kennel in the sky. The postman said that wasn't necessary, but due to compensation rules, he would have to report the incident. He also said the post office would require a letter of apology and reassurance that the dog would be kept under control before further mail could be delivered.

Now, bureaucracy and me never were on the same wavelength, so writing a straight letter of apology would have been a fate worse than no mail. The letter I wrote was as follows (and I quote verbatim): "It pains me greatly to write regarding my dog Cisco biting the letter carrier. Seeing as he brings me mostly junk mail and bills, I had seriously considered getting a larger dog. Yours sincerely."

Believe it or not, that did it. The mail delivery continued, and Cisco lived to scare the hell out of several more mailmen.

Leon's Little Pet

*L*eon, a recent immigrant from Belgium, was renting a small house in Lynn Valley, a suburb at the foot of Grouse Mountain in North Vancouver. Lynn Valley in the early fifties was pretty much trees, birds, squirrels, raccoons, deer, bear, cougar and all the other things that live in the bush.

Leon and his wife Dianne thought they were in paradise. They were especially fascinated by all the wild animals that shared their backyard. One day Leon hollered over the fence to his neighbour, a longtime Lynn Valley resident named Bill, to come see what he had trapped inside his back porch. Leon thought it might make a pet.

Wild critters were old hat to Bill, but he agreed to go have a look. One glance through Leon's screen door, however, and Bill was off like a scalded cat, laughing hysterically. "What's so damn funny?" asked Leon.

"You dumb bastard, that cute little pet you got trapped in there is a skunk."

"What's so funny about a skunk?"

Bill explained the skunk's unique defence mechanism. Meanwhile Dianne, hearing all the commotion, opened the back door that led to the porch. Bill hollered for her to get out of the house by the front door.

"So what do we do now?" asked Leon.

"What do you mean *we*," said Bill. "Skunks are not my specialty. It's your pet, you saw him first." Bill did suggest that if they opened the porch door, the skunk might come out on his own. So Leon opened the porch door and, as planned, the skunk walked through the door. The only problem was, he walked through the wrong open door and was now inside the living room.

"Now what, Bill?"

"Maybe if you take a broom and kind of guide him out real gentle like . . ."

Well, whatever Leon did, it wasn't to the skunk's liking: the critter let fly by the sofa. Right then and there, Leon figures this isn't the best choice for a pet. Hell, he didn't even think it was cute anymore. Dianne ran next door, eyes burning, barfing every few feet. The skunk simply ambled out the back door and into the bush.

"Bill, what the hell do we do now?"

"Go to the store and buy a couple gallons of tomato juice. It's the only thing that works. Not perfect, but it works."

Four or five gallons and a couple of months later, the house was just barely tolerable. For a long time afterwards Dianne was known as the Tomato Juice Kid. As for Leon, he quit collecting pets, at least the ones that are black with white stripes.

Piles, Purgatory and Hell

I've never had the privilege of knowing about piles firsthand, but friends tell me they're what inspired Johnny Cash to record that great hit tune with those immortal words, "burnin' ring of fire."

Now, purgatory I do know about. It's where you do a little burning for minor infractions like "theft under," "undue care," "driving while suspended," or "failing to blow." In purgatory, the fire only gets to your knees, well below your public area, and it's just barely tolerable. But you take hell, now you're really smokin'.

I spent a whole week in hell one time, and this is where the pile drivers come in. My friend Harry ran a pile driver. Actually, Harry was a crane operator—pile drivers sort of run themselves. They're an invention of the devil, spewing smoke and oil and making enough noise to peel paint.

One day, Harry called and said they needed a truck on-site to backfill footings for a large parking lot adjoining a department store in North Vancouver. At the time, I owned and operated a dump truck and was glad for the work.

The site covered an area of about half a city block. In that space, there were a Cat, two backhoes, three compressors and at least a hundred men, plus three huge mobile cranes. Jammed into that mayhem were three of those monster pile drivers.

If you've never worked alongside a pile driver, you've missed a thrill equivalent to a root canal, sans freezing. Piles are often made of reinforced concrete, fifty feet long and one and a half feet thick. The crane lifts the piles on end and places them in a kind of cradle contraption below the pile driver. The pile driver itself is a very simple engine—that is, if you can call a single slab of steel weighing eight tons an engine. The impact of this single diesel-fired piston, which sits directly atop the pile, drives the pile down.

To start the engine, the crane lifts the huge piston up about six feet and drops it. After that, it keeps running as long as fuel is supplied. The noise from this engine plus the impact noise is deafening. The engine throws out massive sprays of oil that cover everything below, and it belches enormous blasts of black smoke every stroke. To keep the top of the concrete pile from shattering, a ten-inch layer of laminated plywood (called a "cookie") sits between the pile and the piston. The cookie becomes saturated from the oil spray, and friction from the tremendous impact sets the cookie on fire. But it really can't burn, as each successive stroke puts out the flame, so it just smoulders, giving off acidic, oily smoke.

When the pile reaches bedrock, or the point of refusal, part of it invariably sticks up too high. Holes are then jackhammered into the area where the pile is to be cut off, dynamite is placed in these holes, and a huge steel barrel is lowered over the pile. Then the top is blasted off. Believe me, there's nothing quite like the sound of dynamite blasting concrete inside a steel barrel.

Now, when you add up three pile drivers, compressors, concrete drilling, blasting, burning plywood, diesel fumes, hot spraying diesel oil, rock dust, and dynamite fumes, not even a self-respecting devil would work in a hellhole like that.

I said to Harry later, "It sure makes you appreciate the loons on a quiet lake in the Cariboo, and as soon as I get my hearing aids from WCB, I'll be able to tell you what they sound like."

Harry said, "Pardon me?"

The Pinto's Last Rites

After losing much of its virtual monopoly of the automobile industry to the Japanese, the Ford Motor Company decided, "If you can't beat 'em, join 'em." Feeling the heat, Ford—along with Chrysler and GM—was forced to enter the small car market, often with disastrous results.

One of Ford's more unfortunate experiments was a car called the Pinto. It was named after a pretty little horse, but that's as far as the resemblance went: it was an undersized, underpowered, poorly finished job that also had a nasty habit of burning up (usually with its inhabitants) when hit from the rear. This was due to a poorly engineered placement of the gas tank near the rear axle housing. The car, however, did have a couple of redeeming factors. It was cheap to buy, and it was cheap to run.

Bill, a school teacher and long-time friend, liked those two redeeming factors. One day, years ago, he showed up with a spanking new Pinto. I lied and said it was a damn fine car and the colour was great. Actually the colour resembled newborn calf shit. But what does a school teacher know anyway? Over the years, Bill babied that Pinto, got pretty good performance, and was, all in all, quite satisfied.

One day Bill showed up with his car. "My Pinto's getting old," he said.

"That sometimes happens," I replied.

"But I really like it, and I want to see if I can get it over two hundred thousand miles."

"Bill, you're one hell of an optimist. What kinda mileage is on it now?"

"One hundred and forty thousand," he said smugly. "I was wondering if you wanted a little backyard work once in a while." I still had my hand tools from my days as a mechanic and said okay. Bill drove off, trailing a slight blue haze. I hoped the old Pinto would die peacefully in her sleep one night and that would be that. No such luck.

A couple of months later, Bill shows up and says the car is running rough. First I check the odometer: one hundred and sixty-nine thousand miles. Then I check the plugs. They look as though they came with the car, the electrodes are nonexistent. I also check the compression. It isn't high, but all the cylinders are equal. So I put in some plugs, a set of points, a gas filter, a new air filter, and fire it up. It runs like a breeze. Happy to see his baby healthy again, Bill pays and leaves.

A year and a half later, Bill drove—or I should say crawled—up to my shop. Never in my life have I heard a car sound so bad, yet still run.

"See what you can do," he said, leaving before I could tell him his baby was gonna need holy water, maybe even extreme unction. Through all those years, the salt on the roads had all but consumed his old car. The fenders were flopping, the quarter panels were rusted out, the rear end was rough and the doors were hanging. But it was the motor that was in the worst shape. I think the cam shaft had gone flat and the main bearing was on its way out. Yes, the Pinto had just had its last ride. The only things worth salvaging were the dash gauges and the plastic front grille, which had survived the salt. I took out the dash gauges and set them in a piece of hardwood with a hook in the back so it could be hung on the wall. It looked real smart!

Later that day, Bill phoned and asked about the Pinto. I said I hadn't had a chance to look at it yet. Right after Bill phoned, I rang my friend Dave, who lived with his wife Yvonne in a beautiful little cove called Batchelor Bay, not far from Horseshoe Bay in West Vancouver. "Are you guys gonna be home tonight?" I asked.

"Hang on, I'll check with Yvonne," he said, and there was a pause. "Yeah, we're going to be home. Are you coming out?"

"Maybe," I answered. "Have you got any church music?"

"I think so."

"Hell, Dave, you got a thousand tapes, you gotta have some organ music."

"I'll check, but why church music?"

"You got any candles?"

"Do bears shit in the woods? Trees are always blowing down on the power lines out here. Everybody has candles. Now would you mind telling me what the hell's going on?" I said I'd tell him later and hung up.

Then I called Bill. "Have I got a deal for you," I said. One thing about Bill, he's a sucker for a deal. He was tailor-made for P.T. Barnum. I could almost hear his wheels spinning over the phone.

"What kinda deal?" he asked impatiently.

"Bill, it's so damn good I can't tell you over the phone. We can't lose. How about meeting us at Dave and Yvonne's place at seven-thirty? I'll give you all the details tonight."

"Okay," he said. "I'll see you there."

It was four-thirty. I phoned Dave back, and he said he'd found a piece that sounded like the stuff they play at a funeral. "Great," I said. "Have you got any wine?"

"I got a couple bottles."

"I'll bring a couple more, just in case. We'll see you guys at seven o'clock."

"Do you mind telling me what's happening?" he persisted. "Is somebody getting married or something?"

I told him that reminded me of the time I said to my girl

friend, "Let's get married or something," and she said, "Let's get married or nothing."

"That's pretty funny," Dave commented. "The first time I heard it I fell right out of my crib. Now cut the bullshit, and tell me what's happening."

"Tell you later. See you at seven," I said, and hung up.

Now, to work. I rummaged through the junk in my shop. Some people wonder why I keep all that stuff, but what sterile, orderly type of workshop would contain enough styrofoam to fashion a tiny coffin in which to place the Pinto's dash gauges? Or enough to make a lid and a small cross? Not many, I bet. Nor would they have a little flat black with which to paint the coffin.

When I was finished, I went inside and Midge and I got dressed. I dug out my ancient black suit, and she found a black dress, black shoes and all. We picked up a couple of bottles of wine and hit Dave and Yvonne's about six-thirty. After we explained the plans and knocked back a couple of drinks, Dave found a small, low table, which we placed in the centre of the room. We placed the coffin on top. It was very solemn-like.

The tension was building. The wine started working and the women were giggling.

"You turkeys better do all your laughing before Bill gets here," I said, " 'cause this is serious business."

We knew Bill would be late—he's the type who will be late for his own funeral. So when I told him seven-thirty, I knew eight-thirty would be the very earliest. That's why we needed the extra wine. We were having one hell of a time, so we tried a little practice run. We lit the candles, pulled the shades, doused the lights and tried the tape. It was perfect.

By eight-ten, Dave had opened yet another bottle of wine. Meanwhile, the women had both found shawls to place on their heads to kind of add a mark of respect. Time was dragging, and they were still giggling. I was wondering how hard a fella would have to rap 'em on the noggin to keep 'em quiet for an hour or two.

Finally, headlights came up the driveway. We cut the lights

and drew the shades. The candles were already lit. After a few minutes, Dave hollered for Bill to let himself in. The funeral music was playing as Bill walked up the stairs to see us all standing, heads bowed around that little casket.

I stepped forward, shook his hand, and said I was sorry. I had done everything humanly possible. Then the others walked over and shook his hand, offering their condolences. For a couple of giggly dames, the women did a fine job of keepin' straight.

I asked Bill if he would like to view the remains. He opened the coffin slowly and lifted out the gauges in their hardwood case. "Bill," I said. "At least she's not suffering anymore."

Bill read the mileage on the odometer of his beloved Pinto: 196,482 miles.

Bill's beloved Pinto odometer still hangs on his apartment wall—and he doesn't bring me any more cars to fix.

Shortcut to the Teahouse

Surrounding Stanley Park and protecting it from the wind and tides is the famous seawall, where thousands of Vancouverites stroll and cycle winter and summer. It's a beautiful walk that takes about two hours to complete, provided you don't get killed by one of the kamikaze skateboarders or cyclists whose sole purpose in life is to terrorize senior citizens.

One sunny Sunday my wife suggested we walk the seawall. It sounded great to me, so we headed over the Lions Gate Bridge, drove through the park to Second Beach and parked the car. Heading westerly, we walked past ships anchored in English Bay waiting for berth space inside the harbour, and watched hundreds of small sailboats off Spanish Banks. Along the seawall there were plenty of kids, bikes and dogs, as well as hundreds of swimmers and sun worshippers, who obviously hadn't read— or didn't believe—all the latest information on the damage of too much sun exposure.

As we approached the south pier of the bridge, we both commented that we were a little hungry. The Prospect Point Teahouse and Restaurant, which is on a ridge overlooking the wall, seemed like a good place to get a bite. The only problem was that, by trail, it was a couple of miles to the restaurant. As the crow flies, however, it was only a couple of thousand yards away.

Now, when you come from Gopher Hole, Saskatchewan, where you had to walk three miles to school every day, the shortcut becomes part of life. My dad called it downright laziness. Little did he realize the gigantic mental strain involved with trying to save those few steps, or the added hazard of cutting through our neighbours' field, where cranky Holstein bulls were at large. Our parents just didn't appreciate all the trials and tribulations us kids had to go through.

Another thing about people from Gopher Hole. They have problems figuring out elevations—hills and mountains and stuff. Anyway, that's what I told people was my excuse for indulging in climbing ventures that weren't conducive to collecting my old-age pension.

Old habits die hard. I took a look at the ridge and said, "Let's take a shortcut and climb the hill to the teahouse."

"Good idea," said my wife.

Running up in the general direction of the teahouse from the seawall was a fairly accessible ravine. At least it looked accessible from our perspective. I did notice, however, that near the top of this ravine we would have to cross over what looked like a bit of a hairy wet portion of ground, due to a rock overhang on the right side of the gully.

We started climbing single file, with me leading. (This was before women's lib. In retrospect, I wish it had been after.) The first two hundred yards or so was fairly easy going, though a lot steeper than it looked from the bottom. The view of the North Shore mountains was getting better by the yard, the people walking and running on the seawall below were getting smaller, the underside of the Lions Gate Bridge was getting larger. I'm thinkin', maybe next year Mount Everest, or at least something that has a little snow on top.

Soon, I notice that the moss we are climbing on is getting a lot wetter and the crossover portion—a hundred yards farther up–looks pretty damn hazardous. Another fifty yards, and the moss we are climbing on starts to tear off the rock face with each step. This shortcut plan doesn't look like such a great idea after all.

Another twenty feet, and we came to the place where the cliffs to the right made it impossible to proceed unless we crossed over to the other side of the ravine. But the centre of the ravine was covered in a green slime, making that route totally impossible. There we were, hanging on the rock, stuck.

I looked down. I couldn't believe how high we were. How in the hell did I do something this damn stupid? I knew we had to start down and I knew that at one stage we were going to slip and tumble all the way down to the seawall, if not right into the chuck. If we got that far without getting killed, I'd probably hear the ambulance men saying, "What do you think you were doing? Only dumb teenagers do this kind of stuff."

I could see the headlines: "Two People Die Scaling Cliffs In Stanley Park," "Middle-Aged Couple Severely Injured," etc. (How dare they call us middle-aged?)

I tried one more step, and everything started sliding off the rock. I said to Midge, who was hanging on in a death grip directly beneath me, "We have to start down."

"I can't move," she said.

"Just take a few inches at a time," I pleaded. "Try and keep in your old tracks. And don't look down."

"I can't do it."

"You have to, it's too damn dangerous for me to try to get around you."

She said simply, "I can't."

The old Saskatchewan Kid was learning a couple of things pretty fast. The first was, it's one hell of a lot easier to climb up rock faces than down. The other thing was, if he lives through this, the next time he goes rock climbing he'll do the chivalrous thing and say, "after you, madame." The one positive part of our situation was that if, or when, we fell, the odds seemed good we'd take a couple of those skate or cycle nuts with us. We wouldn't die in vain.

But we couldn't put off the inevitable forever. So I started to move down in brand new territory, inch by inch, trying to get the tiniest foot- or handhold on that moss-covered rock. It was enough to make me contemplate murdering my everlovin'. When I did finally scramble below my wife, getting her to take a first step must have taken at least twenty minutes.

By the time we got back down to the seawall, we were soaking wet and covered in mud and green slime. Our epic journey had taken over an hour. The people jogging looked at us as though we had just come up out of the sea. The solid pavement sure felt good under our feet.

We walked up to the teahouse—this time no shortcut—and ordered from the take-out booth—we were much too dirty to go inside. Then Midge said the strangest thing I ever heard: "That's the best time I ever had in my life."

You figure it out.

Pet Rock, Skookum Size

"**S**kookum," for the benefit of those poor underprivileged devils who don't happen to live on the BC coast, is an Indian word meaning "big" or "strong." Dead centre on my front lawn in North Vancouver, sits a rock—a pet rock skookum size. It's a little dish-shaped beauty weighing at least eight tons.

Now, this little nugget didn't surf a glacier onto my lawn, nosirree—it got there the hard way. My old friend Bert, who had a bulldozer business, was digging a basement for a new house when he came across this stone. At first he thought he had struck the base of Hollyburn Mountain, but after a half-hour of excavating, this smooth, round monster started taking shape. I was working with Bert at the time, moving fill material across the street. "You know, Bert," I said, "that thing would make a hell of a pet rock." The Lord knew I was kidding; Bert didn't.

"Okay," he said, "let's load 'er up."

Two hours later, the rock was in my ten-ton dump truck. Bert had a 450 Cat, which is a fair-sized machine, but there was no way in the world he could ever lift that baby, or even get a hold of it. So I took the tailgate off the dump box, Bert built a ramp out of fill, and I backed my truck tight against the ramp. While I sat there with my foot on the air brakes, Bert rassled that monstrosity up into the truck. It fit with less than an inch on either side.

I drove back to my house in North Van, backed up onto the centre of my front lawn and lifted the box. After a long pause, out came that eight-ton rock, jumping the truck ahead like a bucking bronco. When I walked around the back, I discovered that the rock had landed on edge, digging into the lawn a good foot. I made a huge plywood sign saying PET ROCK and stuck it in the lawn beside the rock.

When my wife walked in the back door a couple of hours later I said, "I bought you a present. I didn't wrap it, I hope you don't mind."

"What is it?" she asked.

"A rock," I replied.

"A rock?"

"Yes, a pet rock."

"Where is it?"

"On the front lawn."

She walked out the front door and damn near fell down laughing. "Couldn't you find a smaller one?" she said. "What the devil are we going to do with it?"

I said, "It's your rock. You figure what to do with it."

So the rock still sits on my front lawn, growing old graciously. We planted flowers around it, and an artist friend of mine painted an owl and some trees on it. It looks fine and makes a wonderful conversation piece. It's also the only thing I don't have to insure for theft.

Fishing with Tony

My sister Eileen's son-in-law Tony is on the phone from Nanaimo. "I have Friday off. How about coming over and we go fishing?"

"Great idea," says I. "I'll come over on the ferry Thursday afternoon, spend the night at Eileen's, and you can pick me up in the morning. You ain't one of those crazy bastards that go out in the water before daylight to catch them springs before they're fully awake are you?"

"Hell no," Tony answers. "I'll pick you up around eight-thirty."

Thursday is a rare cloudless winter day, and the trip over to Nanaimo is real pleasant. My sister meets me as I walk off the boat, and we spend an enjoyable evening banging out a few tunes on the guitar and the old upright. Now, I'm talking about music that makes sense, such as "Mairzy Doats," "A Boop Boop Dittum Dadum Waddum Chew," "Hutzat Rallston Sittin' On a Rillaragh." God, they just don't write immortal lyrics like that any more.

Next morning, Tony arrives at eight sharp. It's a cold, crisp morning with the first frost of the year. Tony comments about

how there's black ice on the roads and how slippery and
dangerous my sister's new porch is with its invisible skin of clear
ice. On the way down to the water, we make a small detour to
a sporting goods store where I promptly find some hooks for
the killer plugs that my friend Al, the commercial fisherman, had
lent me.

Down we go to the docks. I know I'm safe in the hands of
a cautious captain because Tony drives real careful. We park the
van and Tony takes the rods and the landing net while I carry a
small plastic tub filled with rain gear, a thermos of coffee, a
bottle of rum—that's in case of hypothermia—rubber boots and
those killer plugs.

Just prior to leaving the truck, I tell Tony of my amazing
ability to jinx every fishing expedition invented by mankind.

"That's good," Tony says. "You have a negative attitude
about it and I have a negative attitude also, and two negatives
make a positive, so we'll go out and knock the shit outa them
springs." I'm about to argue, but hell, Tony is a teacher going
for his Masters, so I figure he knows everything about negative
and positive. It's painful, but sometimes a man has to give over
to higher learning.

The tide is out, and the ramp down to the floats is mighty
steep. It's also white with frost. Now, these ramps are all pretty
much made in a standard fashion—half the ramp is smooth
planking so stuff can be wheeled up and down, and the other
half has cleats nailed on every foot or so, so you can walk down
when it's wet or frosty. That way you ain't cluttering up all them
emergency wards. At least that's how my six-year-old grandson
Travis explained it to me.

"Man, we sure the hell better walk down them cleats this
morning," says I, as I see Tony heading for the smooth part of
the ramp. I know he's having a little fun with me, and he's gonna
move over in the last second. I mean, we ain't dealin' with some
green kid from Gopher Hole, Saskatchewan here, we're dealing
with a seasoned sailor and a teacher besides. I know everything
is gonna be cool.

One millisecond later my theory gets blown all to hell. The captain takes one and one-third steps on that smooth planking and instantaneously resembles a 747 touching down—just when the tires go "eek" on the tarmack. Away he goes. Trouble is, Tony doesn't have enough airspeed or wingspan. I'm thinking him being a teacher and all, he may just have wanted to prove to me how Newton's law really works. I know there are exceptions to every rule, but Tony gave me graphic proof that old Isaac wasn't as dumb as he looked.

Tony has what may be described as a hard landing. He lies there, dead quiet. "Look Tony," I think, "you proved your point. I know I'm only a dumb truck driver, and I appreciate what you're trying to teach me, but I already heard about that 'apple on the head' bullshit in school. I'm old, but hell, gravity was invented before I was even born."

Strange how time flies when you're having fun. Tony is still quiet. I don't dare laugh in case he can kick.

"Tony, my fallen captain," I say, "look on the bright side. You coulda slid right under that pipe railing and gone straight down into eighteen feet of water and you might have been carrying Al's killer plugs and lost them. Then we would have been in real trouble." Like a lot of fishermen, Al is touchy about his gear.

Well, Tony figures he's put on that silent-suffering act long enough. He pulls himself up on the pipe railing and hobbles down the rest of the ramp (on the cleats) doing a pretty fair Chester impersonation from the old Matt Dillon series. A one-legged captain on a sailboat called *Pig*. Man, it looked to me like them spring salmon were gonna sleep in their own beds that night.

Conference time. We decide that in the interest of preserving the spring salmon species we should go back home, put some ice on Tony's fast-swelling ankle and get on the inside of that bottle of rum. That's another thing I mentioned to Tony— what a lucky break for us he wasn't carrying the rum when he did that one-and-a-half gainer, booze being so damn expensive and all.

We get back to his house and have a couple of drinks. But Tony is in pain and can't really get into the Christmas spirit. "I have another problem," he says.

"Hell, you got one good leg," I replied, "what more does a man need?"

"You don't understand," he says. "My wife Sandy has a $150 hotel room booked in Victoria for this evening. She may not think this whole damn scene is as funny as you do."

Tony proves to me again how tough he really is. He phones Sandy, who is also a teacher, and quotes a line from Shakespeare's *Julius Caesar*, which roughly translates, "If it had to be done, best it were done quickly." Sandy, it turns out, is very sympathetic and understanding about the whole matter. I didn't hear everything she said, but I do remember her parting expression of love, "If this ever happens again, I'll kill ya."

Tony hangs up and says, "If you think it's so damn hilarious, you can put my snow tires on for me." That sobers me up a little, plus the fact we're running out of rum. I mean, I can get serious if I have to.

Next thing, my sister shows up with a pair of crutches for her son-in-law. So there's poor old Tony with a bag of frozen peas on his ankle, listening to his favourite music, drinking the last of my rum and soaking up all kinds of attention from his mother-in-law. Meanwhile, I'm out in the rain getting a hernia changing his snow tires. Could be this teacher is a little foxier than I thought.

Eventually Sandy comes home from work and she and Tony hit the road for Victoria. "Even if you were in an iron lung, no bloody way am I goin' to lose our hundred and fifty bucks on the hotel room," said Sandy. A very practical woman.

They leave Nanaimo in a real rainstorm, but by the time they start gaining altitude on the Malahat it's turned into a heavy snowstorm. Traffic comes to a complete stop for an hour. All they can do is sit and listen to the radio. But come time to move again, nothing. Their battery is dead.

With horns blaring and a blizzard raging, Sandy starts walking back through the line of cars looking for someone with jumper cables. About the twentieth car back, she hits pay dirt. This good samaritan pulls up alongside the van and gets out his jumper cables. But what do you know, they're a couple of feet too short.

Not to worry, the fella has an ingenious idea. He joins the two cables together to form one long cable, each end to a battery, and runs the vehicles together so the front bumpers are touching. Well, as old Robbie Burns used to say, "The best-laid plans often fall in the crapper." Maybe it was the paint on the bumpers, the atmospheric pressure or the alignment of the planets, but nothing works. The samaritan decides he's had enough of playing in the snow and leaves for Victoria. Tony is trying to get into the lotus position and go "Ommmm," but his leg is too sore. Meanwhile Sandy is secretly wondering whether she could get by on a widow's pension.

Now, here we have the combined brainpower of not one, but two teachers in a confined space. Something has to happen. Sure enough, a light comes on. They are stalled on an incline. They have a stick shift vehicle. They know how to pop the clutch to get the engine going. (Tony remembered when he used to steal his dad's car by letting it roll silently down the driveway and dropping the clutch when the sound of the motor would not be heard by the old man.) Downhill they go. The motor starts, and off they head for the big city. Praise Allah.

Next morning Tony hobbles around Victoria meeting in-laws and people with new babies and all that kind of stuff, but his ankle is still killing him. So his buddy finally talks him into going to the emergency ward for an X-ray. Lo and behold, he has a fracture above the ankle. Now he has a place on his leg for people to sign their names and draw little funny pictures and things. Sandy gets the fun of driving the van back over the Malahat, through another snowstorm, to Nanaimo. And other than coming on the scene of a fiery head-on collision—with dead and injured people—the trip is uneventful. The next week, for relaxation, Sandy goes bungee jumping.

As soon as Tony gets his cast off, we'll once again attempt to challenge the wild sea, before all them poor spring salmon die of old age.

"One other thing, Tony," I cracked as I rolled out of the driveway, "this time two negatives didn't make a positive."

I'm sure I heard Sandy remark, "Tony, would you mind if we had an unlisted number?"

Band-Aids Under the Bridge

The phone rang. It was Bob, a friend I'd worked with in the excavation and trucking business. He had just bought a twenty-six foot pleasure boat and asked if I would like to go for a little ride with him to Horseshoe Bay. It was a warm, bright day, and I hadn't planned anything in particular, so I said, "Sure." Bob said to meet him at the Mosquito Creek Marina at ten o'clock.

The Mosquito Creek Marina is a few blocks west of Lonsdale Avenue in North Vancouver, directly across the BC Railway tracks from the famous twin-spired St. Paul's Catholic Church. The church is a landmark in North Van that dates back to the time of the great Vancouver fire. Just a single spire at the time, it was the only thing the Squamish Indians were able to see through the smoke as they paddled their canoes over to rescue people trapped by the fire on the Vancouver side of Burrard Inlet.

I met Bob just before ten and we walked down the dock to where his new—at least new to him—boat was docked. The boat was called the *Miss Sointu*, "Sointu" being short for Sointula, a small Finnish fishing village off the northern tip of Vancouver Island, on Malcolm Island.

The boat looked in good shape. The fiberglass-over-ply-wood hull had been freshly painted and there was a brand-new canvas cover over the aft end. The six-cylinder Chev that powered the boat was of unknown vintage. But Chev has been making reliable six-cylinder engines since the twenties so we didn't think there should be any worries in that department. The engine had just been tuned, too. We were ready to sail, or rather, motor off into the sunset.

Bob started the engine and I cast off the lines. We moved slow and easy out into Burrard Inlet, heading for the First Narrows. The tide was just starting to go out, the sea was flat, and there were lots of pleasure craft heading out to catch that trophy to hang on the wall. (Sometimes I think sportfishermen are as crazy as prairie wheat farmers—they're always after the big fish or the big crop.)

Just as we passed under the Lions Gate Bridge, at the point where the Capilano River enters the sea, that reliable old Chev (with the recent tune-up) quit. Just like that, no bucking or coughing, no warning. She just up and died.

Bob tried the starter a few times. Nothing. I said, "Now, you wouldn't have come out here and done something stupid like run out of gas, would you?"

"Hell no," Bob snapped back, "I fuelled up last night."

We started drifting toward the rocks at the mouth of the river. Bob, understandably, was worried about damaging his new boat. As for myself, I wasn't looking forward to a swim in that cold water. I pulled off one of the spark plug leads, held it near the block, and asked Bob to try the starter. Not even a ghost of a spark. I figured the ignition points must have closed up, as sometimes happens if they are not tightened down on the plate in the distributor. I snapped off the distributor cap, aware we were drifting closer to the rocks.

One look and I knew we were in trouble. "Holy Christ, Bob. This is serious. The bloody rotor is broken in half." The rotor is a small plastic and metal gadget that sits on top of the distributor shaft. Its purpose—that is, when it's not lying at the bottom of the distributor in two pieces—is to rotate and distribute the spark from the coil to the individual spark plugs.

"I'm gonna call the Coast Guard," said Bob, " 'cause in another few minutes, we're gonna be right on top of those rocks."

"Not a bad idea," I answered, "but by the time they get here, you and I are gonna need a couple of them new-fangled things they call flotation devices—you know those red things that look almost like life jackets."

Bob looked like a crew member on the *Titanic*, after it hit the iceberg. I asked if he had any friction tape.

"Nope."

"Any fine wire, stove pipe, copper, haywire, anything like that?"

"Nope."

"Damn. What the hell kinda sailor are you anyway?"

Bob didn't answer, he was too busy trying to raise the Coast Guard on the radio. With the hundreds of boats out, the Coast Guard was more than likely busy elsewhere. By this time, I could hear the waves slapping and washing over the rocks and I knew we were in too far for any other boat to get near us safely.

Panic time. I said, "Bob have you got a first aid kit?"

"I think there's one in that pull-out drawer under the table."

I yanked open the drawer and grabbed the first aid kit. There wasn't a single inch of adhesive tape—just some gauze, iodine, Q-tips and a couple of those stretchy Band-Aids. Desperate for something, I grabbed the bandaids, tore off the gauze patches and wrapped the two little pieces of stretch tape around the broken rotor. Then I stuck the rotor back on the distributor shaft and snapped the distributor cap back on.

"Bob," I said, "try that starter. And if you're a religious man, this might just be the time for you to do a little prayin'." By now the rocks were close enough to touch with a pike pole.

Bob tried the starter. That old Chev revved right up, nice as pie. It never even faltered when he slipped her into reverse and backed away. We travelled slowly about a quarter mile to the dock in West Van, where we tied up and went looking for a new rotor.

Bob thought I was a bloody genius, but, hell, it wasn't that at all. I just have a little talent for haywiring. And a deep fear of cold water.

The Parts Department

With the present shop labour rate at fifty dollars an hour, I don't make a practice of heading for a garage every time my truck breaks wind or passes a little water. Particularly since I own a full set of hand tools and have broached some of the mysteries of the infernal combustible motor. However, the asthmatic attacks and gasping seizures of my motor were becoming so frequent that I decided to limp down to the garage, have a scope check put on, and live happily motor-wise ever after.

My truck was of 1964 vintage, which was probably the reason most of the mechanics hid under their benches or fled to the washroom as I sputtered to a halt in front of a door marked SERVICE ENTRANCE.

A man in a meticulous white smock approached warily upwind and walked nervously around the truck three times, sniffing out serial and model numbers and joking weakly about a possible terminal illness.

"They don't build them like they used to," I volunteered.

"Allah be praised," was his smartassed reply.

"Sign here." he said. "Go have a coffee, and I'll have Jerry put it on the scope."

When I returned the tuneup man said, "You need plugs, a carb overhaul and a fuel pump."

"Go ahead," I said to his amazement.

Just before closing, I left a cheque for three hundred and fifty-eight dollars and sixty-three cents.

Two blocks later, the truck went into a violent coughing spell, passing some gas, followed by a violent explosion which ruptured the muffler. I realized I was three hundred and fifty-eight dollars and sixty-three cents poorer but still had a sick truck, plus a blown-out muffler. I limped back to the garage to find total darkness. The inhabitants had fled, perhaps to South America.

Now us prairie boys learn pretty quick, so I wasn't about to spend another small fortune just to have somebody cast aspersions on my pride of the fleet—actually the total fleet—one 1964 "never driven by an old lady" dump truck.

"Do it yourself," my mother used to say.

Next day I purchased a new muffler and tail pipe, and without invoking the name of the Lord too profusely, installed them on the truck. Now I still had a sick truck, but at least it was a quiet sick truck.

My truck and I went back to work, but two days later she died, with a load on her back, at a picturesque village overlooking Howe Sound called Lions Bay, some twenty-five miles from Vancouver. Take it cool, I said to myself, no sense getting excited. Then I called a pox on the house of all tuneup men, and began frothing at the mouth.

Now there's a black, round, inert object that sits next to the distributor, called a coil. Well, this little object started to intrigue me, mostly due to the fact it was the only damn thing that hadn't been replaced.

Next morning, after hitching a ride home with the loader operator, I borrowed a coil from another trucker friend and drove back to Lions Bay. Five minutes later, with the other coil installed, the truck started instantly and has been running like a Swiss watch ever since. So much for scope checks and tuneup mechanics. I now felt like I could walk across Howe Sound, or at least the Deas Island Slough, without my water skis.

Two days later, my truck started running a fever and losing bladder control. I don't mind losing a little water from time to time, but when that water is half antifreeze at ten bucks a gallon, my one-eighth Scottish ancestry starts kicking in.

Do it myself, said I, so out came the radiator—a surprisingly simple procedure. Four hours and sixty-four dollars later, I replaced the rad, all patched and painted with a black tar-like substance that dries in just twelve and a half years.

Filled with thirty dollars worth of antifreeze, I was once again ready to face the world—the world being a six-hour job at the University of British Columbia, twenty-odd miles from home.

Next morning at six-thirty, with the temperature below freezing, I embarked for the halls of higher learning to do a patch-up re-paving job on one of the student parking lots. Halfway to the job, on a street with the unique name of Broadway, my beloved again got the fever—with periodic belches of steam, like Old Faithful. A gnawing suspicion dawned on me that the incontinent condition might be caused by something other than the rad.

Several water stops and six hours later, back on old Broadway, the do-it-yourself craze seized me once more like the Protestant work ethic. I never could figure whether I was afflicted by the Protestant 'work ethic', or the Catholic 'eat ethic'. Nevertheless, my route passed a large truck repair garage, where I entered another world called PARTS DEPARTMENT.

Now those of you who have never ventured into the mysteries of a parts department are leading a shallow, unenlightened existence. One thing should be noted, all parts come in small cardboard boxes. Yes, those were the days before everything was hermetically sealed with plastic that you can only cut with a bloody carbide-tipped skillsaw. I have seen old pensioners die of malnutrition before my cataract-covered eyes, trying to open those damn jam and marmalade things that the cafes give you for breakfast. And the worst part is after you do get the damn thing open, you find that the plastic tastes better than the stuff they put inside.

As I was saying, everything came in cardboard boxes, three inches by four inches. Despite the fact the automobile is made of huge slabs of iron, everything came in little cardboard boxes. Ask for a crank shaft or a rear axle, the parts man reaches for a little cardboard box. Damned puzzling to say the least.

Now most do-it-yourselfers come to the parts confessional booth ill prepared and sore afraid. Parts men have devious methods of trapping the unwary, like asking for year, style, serial number, power steering or manual, auto trans or manual, air conditioning or not, tilt cab or standard, whether the truck was made in Dearborn or Windsor, whether the rear end is an Eaton or Simpson Sears, etc., etc.

Not wishing to be caught short, I always arrive prepared with every conceivable statistic. But not to be outdone, the parts man asks for the paint code or my sign of the zodiac. You can't bloody win. I suppose it's their way of getting even with us for having to remember all those parts numbers.

Anyway, just behind the fan and bolted on the front of the motor sits the water pump, whose job is to circulate the water and not dissipate it on the street in copious quantities. As this now appears to be the culprit, I brazenly step up to the counter and ask for a pump for a model F700, 332 motor, conventional cab, 1964 Ford, serial and model numbers etc., etc.

The parts man reaches for a book weighing one hundred and fifty pounds, a foot and a half thick, and says, "new or rebuilt?"

"What's the difference?"

"Twenty-six dollars."

"I'll take a new one."

"We don't have a new one."

In that case, I'll take a rebuilt.

"We are out of stock, I'll have to order one in," says the parts man. He picks up the phone . . . "High or low fan?" he asks.

"Huh," says I.

Then on the phone, he asks for a C2397D42, a long silence, then "Okay, send one over." Then to me he says, "You can pick it up tomorrow morning, it's Saturday but we stay open till three."

Next morning I phone to see if the rebuilders had sent over the pump. Six calls and six busy signals later, I decide to drive over and pick it up. After waiting in line twenty minutes, I reached the desk. "I ordered a water pump last night, I'm from Cap's Trucking."

"Hey Neil, you order a water pump for Cap's Trucking?"

From back in the maze of bins, a voice calls back, "Those idiots sent two over, both the wrong pumps."

The parts man says to me, "We're in trouble."

Now I knew *I* was in trouble, but what in hell is this *we* stuff?

He picks up the phone. "I'll see if anybody's down at the rebuilders." After a long pause, he hands me the phone.

"This is the answering service, we are closed on Saturdays, if you care to leave a message, wait for the tone and proceed."

I hung up the phone.

Then he said, "I'll try one of the other dealers."

"Check a number, one only C2397D42." A long silence, then "Good, order number 4976, customer will call."

"Good news," he says, "they got one out by the airport on Southwest Marine Drive, you can pay for it here and pick it up." I wanted to kiss the hem of his trousers.

"One more thing, there'll be a ten-dollar core charge."

"A what?"

"A core charge, for your old pump."

"I have the old pump in the pickup."

"Good, bring it in."

When I finally lay the old pump on the counter, he says "That bypass pipe won't come with the rebuilt, see Carl in the shop, he'll take it out for you."

"What about the plug?" I ask.

"No, the plug comes with the rebuilt."

So I go into the garage and a guy is hosing down the floor. "You Carl?"

"No Carl is out road-testing a car."

I walk over to a bench, put the pipe in the vise and screw it out of the pump, put the old pump on the parts counter, pay the cashier eighty-nine dollars and forty-eight cents and head for Marine Drive, ten miles away.

Another lineup at the parts counter—Saturday is not a good day to pick up parts. The parts man takes my piece of paper with the order number, disappears and returns with a pump that doesn't even remotely resemble my old one.

I say "That's not the right—"

He gives me that "how dare you challenge Moses" look and says, "What model was that truck?" I tell him and he opens up a book two feet thick, then says, "Those guys on Broadway sent up the wrong number."

I say "Gee whiz," or something like that.

"Hold on, I'll check and see if we happen to have the right one."

Several minutes later he reappears with a pump in his hand and says, "I got one here, but it looks like it's been brought back. Looks okay to me though, after all, what can go wrong with a water pump?"

I say that's what the captain said about the *Titanic*. I take the pump and the first thing I notice is that the plug that "always comes with the rebuilt" is missing. So back to Broadway to retrieve the plug from my old pump, then home. I should be truckin tomorrow.

With the temperature and night both falling, I decide to get right to it. The pump fits good on the block, so I bolt it all up tight. Next come the fan belts, and I notice that they don't line up with the crankshaft pulley. On closer inspection, I find that the pulleys on the water pump have not been pressed far enough on the shaft, so off with the pump and into my shop, where I "press" those pulleys on with a large hammer. Then I bolt the pump back on and the belts line up fine. When I go to tighten the fan belts, which is accomplished by swinging out the alternator, I find that the alternator won't swing out far enough. The only explanation for this phenomenon must be that the new pump has smaller pulleys than the old one. The only temperature that was falling now was on the Celsius scale.

The solution—try to find shorter fan belts. Six service stations later, no luck with the belts. Meanwhile back at the truck, I take off the alternator adjustment strap, cut it in half and weld a piece in the middle. Some prophetic old turkey once coined that phrase "more haste, less speed," and he was right on.

When I go to put that strap back on I find I'd welded the strap together with the curve going the wrong way. Damn good thing there were no ladies present. So back to the bench, cut the strap again and reverse the curve. Now the belts tighten up fine. Next comes the water pump bypass hose. Here I find that the bypass hose is five-eighths of an inch, while the pipe on the water pump is three-quarters, and there's no way you can force a five-eighths hose over a three-quarter pipe, and Lord knows I tried.

Back down to several gas stations and the same story over and over, "We don't carry that size hose. You must have some oddball car or something."

I try one last garage and the manager says, "We never carry that size hose."

But the mechanic in the back overhears and says, "Sure, we got some three-quarter hose." So I'm quickly with that mechanic. "This hose is expensive as hell," he says.

I said "Go your best lick, you can't hurt me no more today."

Back to the truck with six inches of the world's most expensive hose, and with a fair amount of fiddling and forcing, I manage a Mickey Mouse leakproof bypass system. On with the rad, painted with that never-dry black goop. By now it's pitch black outside and getting real cold.

I fill the rad with antifreeze and all seems okay. Only one small problem—the next time the water pump fails, the whole process will have to be reversed.

Like the man said, "What can go wrong with a water pump?"

II.

Growing Up on the Prairies

Schtoopid Kids

When the Chinooks come blowing out of Alberta, and the black earth starts pushing up through the snow on high ground, Saskatchewan farmers begin dreaming of parking their Stanfields for another season. And as daylight hours lengthen, they wait for the fields to dry in the low spots so they can get back on the land for the coming year.

For us prairie kids, spring meant the first smell of decaying snow and thawing ground, the first icicles on the eaves, and most of all, the very first sound of water on the move. It was a magic time.

It was also the time to check the slough. The slough was a low, bowl-shaped depression in the flats, a hundred yards north of our old swimming hole in the Battle River. All our pastures drained into a coulee that snaked around our house and out-house and down to the slough. When the slough got too high, it would drain into the river. Sometimes during spring breakup the huge slabs of rotting ice would pile up at the river bend and the Battle River would drain back into the slough.

Every day before and after school we ran to the slough, and with a long red willow or a broken hockey stick we would check the height of the water. School days were mighty long in the springtime, when a fella was waiting for the gophers to wake up and the meadowlarks to come back to the fenceposts. Centuries passed, waiting for that damn slough to become navigable.

Water was a rare commodity on prairie farms. Often, when we did see water, it wasn't in the form of life-giving rain, but in a short, devastating hailstorm. My dad had nine wells divined and dug around that farm, but each time when water was finally found it tasted like Epsom salts. "Alkali wells," they were called— the water from them was so foul even the cows wouldn't touch it. Consequently, all the water for our farm, house and stock came from the Battle River.

Well, the cows and horses could damn well walk to the river and get their own water. But for the house, we hauled the water in forty-five-gallon barrels that sat on a low skid contraption called a "stone boat." That was for the winter. In the summer we used a water tank. It was a half-circle affair that fit between the bunks of the farm wagon and held about 250 gallons of water. The water was poured in through a square hole in the top and emptied through a bung at the bottom in the back. The main problem with this tank was that the damn thing leaked, and after a long dry winter, the planks would shrink, and it would pass water as fast as you could dump it in the top.

Now wooden boats, barrels and tanks have one thing in common: they all leak when they are dry. The only cure is water. To tighten the old tank, my dad would place it in the slough. Then as the water rose slowly, the planks would tighten up one by one till she was watertight, or nearly so.

One spring Monday, the old tank started to float. The weather was warm all week, and by Friday the slough was full. Then on Friday night, the temperature dropped like a rock. On Saturday morning, myself, our 6'4" half-breed hired man (with the unlikely name of Bat) and my friend Vic Charbonneau, a "city kid" from Battleford, walked down to the slough.

There was a chill in the air and a half-inch of crystal ice covered the pond. The tank was frozen fast. Hell, that was no tank, that was a ship, and an icebreaker to boot. We scoured the bank and found a couple of poles. We hopped aboard our yacht and put Vic in the middle with his feet dangling in the filler hole, out of the way. Breaking ice around the tank, we poled our craft to the middle of the pond.

Now our ship, without ballast or keel, and being barrel-shaped on the bottom, had to be manoeuvred with extreme delicacy. Bat was no sailor, and no one would ever accuse him of being delicate. But one thing he was good at was scaring the hell out of us kids.

So, good old Bat stands up on that tank and rocks it back and forth. Well, we holler at him to stop, but he only rocks harder and harder. All the while he's wearing a wild look of ecstasy. A couple more rocks and that old tank flips clean over and we go crashing through the ice into eight feet of water.

To call that breathtaking would be the understatement of the century. We headed for shore, the city kid dog-paddling ahead, breaking a trail through the ice. I followed behind, and back of me, killing himself laughing, was good old Bat. If I'd been bigger I would have reached back and gladly drowned the bastard.

We finally made shore. We were safe on dry land at last, but we still had a quarter-mile to get to the house. Man, it was cold! Farther up the hill a hell of a wind was blowing, but Bat was still laughing. No sense, no feeling.

I was thinking about the warm kitchen stove and what Mom would say: "My poor kid, you could have got drownded." Mom was Swiss, and when you cross that with English you don't merely drown, you get drownded.

We crashed through the kitchen door at last, looking like three clear, glazed popsicles. Mom came in from the living room, took one look, and said three words: "You schtoopid kids."

Next time I go to sea, I thought, it won't be on a water tank. Bat won't be allowed above deck either, if he's allowed on board at all. The city kid can stay, in case we ever need someone to break the ice. I also plan to get a new mother who is more in tune with the health and welfare of her third-eldest son. Schtoopid kids, indeed. We could have got drownded.

Louis Caplette

My grandfather was half French, a quarter Cree and a quarter Scotch and Irish. He was always in the background of family life, silent, smoking his pipe and smelling strongly of the Sloan's liniment he rubbed in for his rheumatism. Centre stage was always taken by my half-breed, Scottish, Presbyterian Bible-thumping, fire and brimstone grandmother.

I only knew my grandfather in his old age, when he would walk stiffly around the hollyhock beds beside his log house, walking stick in hand, dangin' this and dangin' that. My grandmother said if he didn't stop that infernal cussin', he would surely bring down the wrath of the Lord. Every week or so, my grandmother would "shave" Grandpa with a pair of scissors, as his eyes had become so bad he was nearly blind and unable to shave himself. This procedure was also carried on with lots of dangin' and complainin'.

In his bedroom, which we were never allowed to enter, sat a dresser with a huge porcelain washbasin, a bottle of Sloan's liniment and the Bible. Under the bed was a porcelain chamber pot and a gallon jug of port. Several times during the night, Grandpa would develop a certain type of cough that could only be relieved by a little shot of that panther piss. Strangest cough I ever did hear. My grandmother said it was the Devil's work, but I don't think that was it.

No, I think the poor old bugger, almost totally blind and getting crippled up with rheumatism, just wanted a little glow so he could drift off to the old times. Like when he was running freight wagons three hundred miles across the prairies, often in minus-forty-degree weather; or when he and his fur-trading father-in-law, Charlie Bremner, were taken prisoner by the Indians for two weeks during the Riel rebellion; or when his father-in-law was charged with treason for aiding and abetting the rebellion; or when he watched helplessly while that arrogant thieving bastard—the then-vaunted Canadian hero, General Middleton—stole four wagonloads of Bremner's furs.

Maybe Grandpa wanted to relive his fifteen-year struggle for justice with the Canadian government—a government headed by that racist old drunk, Sir John A. Maybe he wanted to dream of the time later when, in the Supreme Court of Canada, Charlie finally got paid for the furs, and that crook Middleton was forced to resign in disgrace and return to England, where his "punishment" was to be made keeper of the jewels for the royal family. (Who says crime doesn't pay?)

As a kid, I never knew my grandfather as anything but a cranky, pipe-smoking old man. It was only long after his death that I found out he had been so closely involved with the whole history of the early west. Grandma thought he was a petulant old drunk. Hell, by today's standards, he wouldn't even qualify as a minor social drinker. As Dylan says, the times, they are a changin'.

Grandpa homesteaded a quarter section a couple of miles west of the little French Canadian village of Delmas (so named for one of the early priests in the area). He and Grandma raised ten kids, which was just about average for those times on the prairies. A man needed lots of sons to clear and break the land.

Likely a simple cataract operation would have given him some sight and a lot of comfort in his old age. At least he would have been able to go out and look at the stock: a farmer is in big trouble when he can't look at his stock. Grandpa would say things like, "I seen that roan cow in the pasture this morning and she was bawling for her calf; I wonder if a coyote got that dang calf." But generally his boys just ignored him. I'd think, why in hell doesn't somebody pay attention to this old man? Don't his opinions count for anything?

Part of his frustration surely must have come from being ignored for his opinions or advice. I didn't know at the time, but that's what kids are for. Hell, maybe he did see that roan cow in the pasture—who knows? And what harm would it have done to say, "Okay, I'll go out and check on that cow right after dinner."

It wasn't until long after his death I learned that my grand-father could read and write. And only after reading about him in historical journals of the time did I find that he was fairly well educated, at least for those days.

All the clerical and bookwork for Charlie Bremner's store and fur-trading business was done by my grandfather. On the rare occasion when he did speak, he would generally preface his remarks with, "I tell you what." I think it was meant to sort of give emphasis, probably because he was being ignored so much, and being blind and all.

I only wish I could have talked to him more about the old times and troubles on the prairies, the freighting and fur business and things like that. But Grandma always sort of ran interference. Besides, in those days kids were to be seen and not heard, period.

Sometimes when Grandpa got a little extra port and started singing, Grandma would tell him to be quiet and wonder to herself why God made her put up with such a cussed old man. In her religion, people were supposed to suffer on this earth and get their reward in heaven. I suppose her main concern was how to drag this old sinner up there with her.

When Grandpa died, Grandma followed him within a week, probably to make sure he didn't drink too much of that port under the bed. My hope is that they have a good supply of Sloan's liniment when he gets creaky, and just a touch of port when he gets cranky.

The City Kid Hitches a Tow

The Battle River was two, maybe three hundred feet lower than our barn, so walking the cows down to water was easy going. Climbing back up that hill on a hot day, however, was not our idea of a good time. "Hard work never killed anybody," my mother used to say, and she sure the hell proved that by example. But she was Swiss, and us kids were only half-Swiss, so hard work might well have killed us.

One work-saving device we discovered was a cow's tail, preferably one with the cow attached. When the cows were finished drinking in the river and were snaking back up the hill, we would grab the tail of the last cow. The cow would take off at a run, and we would get towed up the hill. The only trick was to let go just before the top so Dad wouldn't catch us.

Come spring, with the cows feeding on the new grass, they could crap a jet stream straight out, four to five yards. For that reason, we stayed clear of the tow jobs in the spring. I didn't mind taking the odd gamble, but hanging on a cow straining up a hill in springtime? No thanks! The odds were too high.

Now city kids didn't know about such matters, nor was I about to teach them. One spring weekend a city kid was staying with us. After milking, he and I drove the cows down to the river. They tanked up, and we headed them back to the upper pasture. Just as the last cow hit the base of the hill, the city kid grabbed its tail. The cow gave about three big jumps with the kid hangin' on like a bronc buster. Then, BAM!, a total explosion of liquid cow shit!

I thought later of the Jolly Green Giant. Well, that city kid wasn't jolly, but he sure the hell was green, totally covered in hot, gooey, green cow shit. God, what I wouldn't have done for a movie camera! But hell, I couldn't have held a camera still, I was too busy rolling on the ground. I've never seen a funnier sight.

The city kid ran right back to the river and jumped in, clothes and all. I laid on the bank and laughed till my belly was sore.

Whenever the hired man told about a funny incident he'd say, "It was funnier than the time my grandmother got her tit caught in the wringer." Well, to this day, when I think of that kid and the cowshit, it still kills me. It was a lot funnier than getting your tit caught in the wringer, and on that I'll lay odds.

We're Going to Delmas

Delmas was a sleepy French Canadian hamlet of possibly two hundred souls, that is, if you counted noses on Saturday night. The village had a combination post office and general store with livery barn at the rear, three grain elevators, a church and a residential convent for Indian children. Townspeople mostly spoke French, but English was not uncommon.

My grandparents' place was located about two miles from Delmas. This made the total distance from our farm in Battleford about twenty-two miles, an astronomical distance when travelled at twelve to fifteen miles per hour in the back of our Model A pickup truck—especially one that slowed to six miles per hour on the curves. Dad was no Juan Fangio on the highway.

About once a month the tension built up on our farm until my father would announce, as calm as anything, at suppertime, "We're going to Delmas tomorrow." Us kids would burst with excitement and cold fear—some of us would go and some would have to stay and help with chores. After an agonizing pause, my father would announce who could go and which ones had to march to the execution chamber.

Those of us who were chosen received looks of cold steel

from those who weren't, and often tears were shed. When I had to stay, I wished with all my might for a hurricane or an earthquake, or at least a heavy rain, because the last twelve miles of highway to Delmas weren't gravelled and a rain turned the road into a gumbo quagmire. I knew my father wasn't one to take chances with uncertain weather, even though the possibility of rain in that part of the country was about on a par with being hit by lightning.

The evening and night prior to the trip would take a whole lifetime to pass. On this one particular night, we all went to bed early, but I couldn't sleep, partly from excitement and partly from fear of being murdered by my brother (it was his turn to stay). But after prayers for the preservation of the truck, the weather and the health of us kids—at least till the journey got under way—I dozed off.

The prayers held, and the sky was clear next morning. My mother was frantic getting us kids to wear our good clothes and making sure we had all hit the outhouse before departure. As usual, she made sandwiches in case there was trouble on the road.

"Come on, old girl," said my father. Mother reminded him that she was not an old girl and that she had to get all us kids ready, while all he had to do was "smoke that bloody old pipe." Mother finally ushered us aboard while my father checked the oil, filled up the radiator and told us kids to "sit down on the bed of the truck," or we would have to stay home. We sat.

Dad picked up the crank, took the car out of gear, opened the choke rod and lifted the spark lever. Then he told Mother what to do in case the motor started, and she told him where to go. Dad walked around to the front and cranked her over twice, while pulling on the choke wire strung through the radiator. He then let go of the choke, gave her a half-turn, and she burst into life with a cheer from us kids and a look of despair from my brother. Dad choked her a couple of more times to make sure she wouldn't die, then made a dash from the front to the inside, where he sat for a minute adjusting the spark lever while she warmed up.

Then, with a lurch, and with the dogs barking and running alongside till we got to the highway, my dad put the car in high and away we went. Us kids in back were in ecstasy as the farm started to slide from sight, and the dogs finally gave up the chase. When the top of the old house was only just visible, we broke into a violent argument as to who would be the very last one to see the farm. Sometimes, I would stand up quickly, take a final glimpse, and drop down just as quick so my father wouldn't notice. Then I'd hold my sisters down so they couldn't do the same and therefore lay claim to being the last to see the farm, amidst cries of "cheater," and "I'm going to tell Daddy on you."

We proceeded past my uncle's farm a half mile away. While we watched for gophers and beer bottles, Mother sang a Swiss song. The whole countryside had a parched look, and my father said we couldn't pay the mortgage again this year.

Halfway to Delmas was a place called Highgate. It consisted of two elevators and one house; we thought it was a fair-sized town. How it came by that name I couldn't say, but I do remember a sense of keen disappointment when I first saw the place. There wasn't a high gate to be seen. I never placed much faith in place-names after that.

Two miles past Highgate we stopped at Aunt Violet's place for lunch. Vi, as she was generally called, was the most talkative woman I ever knew. She was married to a quiet, ancient, mysterious Frenchman who could sit for hours without uttering a solitary word. The rest of my uncles and aunts always referred to Aunt Vi as "that poor girl." She always seemed cheerful to me and certainly made enough noise to compensate for that silent Frenchman.

After lunch us kids were rounded up for the final lap of the journey. Sometimes Aunt Vi came along with us; her husband never seemed to mind, or if he did, he never said.

After another hour (the last two miles on a wagon trail), we arrived at my grandparents' gate amid barking dogs and aunts, uncles and grandparents coming out to greet us. My grandmother asked us kids if we were good and then gave us all a kiss. When no one was looking, I wiped mine off.

Grandmother was very religious, and us kids were always afraid to commit some cardinal sin in her presence. She was modest to a degree never equalled in modern times and claimed Grandpa had never seen her bare feet.

My grandparents' house had a large kitchen with a trapdoor in the floor and an earthen cellar below where all the preserves, fruit, pickles and whatnot were stored. My uncles used to open the trap and threaten to throw me in. I would be terrified, as there were lizards down there and it was pitch black if the trap was closed.

The livingroom, which was out of bounds except on rare occasions, was up one step and off to the left of the kitchen. It was a long room with several hooked rugs on the well-polished floor. Two violins hung on the wall and at the far end of the room stood an ancient piano, perpetually out of tune, which my aunt Lil used to play. But for me, the centre of attraction was a picture that hung near the piano. It was a wild, exciting picture of a black and white horse terrified by a lightning storm and running wild-eyed with nostrils flared under a black-clouded sky. The picture sort of scared me, but on the few occasions I was allowed in the livingroom, I couldn't stay away from it.

After lunch my father and uncles played the violins and Aunt Lil chorded the piano. My grandmother sang "The Old Rugged Cross," while my mother made certain us kids paid proper attention.

I was never too sure how my mother, being Swiss, a foreigner, a non-Catholic and a widow with three kids when she married my father, was accepted into that strict religious family. I expect it was quite a shock to my grandmother, who put the damper on more than one romance involving her brood. Consequently several of my uncles wound up bachelors. Lucky for me, my dad wasn't one of them. However, my mother had a brutally honest approach that was so direct and sure that she could never long be ignored or discounted. She was badly outnumbered in that family, but us kids knew she could hold her own anywhere.

Soon it was time to leave for home. After many farewells, and the utter confusion that parting always brought, and after several promises to return soon, we piled into the old pickup. One of my uncles twisted her tail while Dad worked the controls. Three times and she started, just like normal. Us kids knew a Ford was the best damn car in the world.

One uncle rode with us on the running board down to the gate and let us through. When we hit the dirt road my dad shifted into high and my mother said, "Could we go a little faster?" We had a long journey ahead.

The Great Gopher War

Their death toll far surpassed the human losses of World War I, World War II and all preceding and later conflicts. They have had to survive heavy artillery, trapping, poisoning, drowning out, shooting, snaring, slingshots, and death on gravel roads under the wheels of Model T and Model A Fords. Hawks, coyotes, weasels, foxes and badgers have also taken their toll. If I was a gopher, and still alive, I would write a book called "Against All Odds."

How the prairie gopher has survived is a mystery. Part of it has to be that they don't have TV, the winters in Saskatchewan are long and they are all Catholics. It could also be that they only read that first chapter in the Bible, saw all that begatting and said, "Man, this sure beats Trivial Pursuit." The gopher was the only critter in Saskatchewan that had more kids than the farmers. You see, the farmers never had TV either, just old radios with dead batteries.

Every time the farmer had a crop that survived grasshoppers, drought, rust and hail, the gopher said, "That's mine." The farmer said, "Over my dead body. No, better still, let's make that over *your* dead body." So the lines were drawn. It was the good guys versus the bad guys. The bad guys (the farmers) petitioned the government for help to rid the prairies of these varmints, and after lots of time and pressure, the government said it would pay the princely sum of one half-cent bounty for gopher tails. That's where us kids came in.

Canadian historians will tell you the fur trade played the major role in the development of Canada. Ask any Saskatchewan kid with a red willow slingshot in his back pocket, and he will let you know in no uncertain terms what built Canada. It was the gopher tail trade, pure and simple.

Now, about slingshots. The first and foremost requirement for a good slingshot was a good crotch, which we pronounced "crutch." If I had a buck for every hour I spent searching for perfect red willow crotches, I'd be driving a Porsche instead of a Datsun. When you see those damn willows from a distance it looks like they have all kinds of perfect crotches. Then when you get up close they're twisted, crooked, of unequal thickness, too large or too small. Whoever said, "The grass is always greener in the distant field," must have apprenticed in slingshot crotch hunting.

To make a good slingshot we also needed rubber, scissors, string and leather. Every prairie boy's idea of heaven was a perfect red willow crotch, tied with red auto tube rubber. I'm talkin' real rubber—the kind that kept all the old Fords a couple inches above the mud, dust and washboard prairie roads, rubber that felt alive in the hand, not that black synthetic crap that stretches a fraction then goes dead as a rope. If us kids had used that synthetic stuff the gophers would have all died of old age. (Mind you, those old glass telephone pole insulators would have had more of a fighting chance.)

The problem was that farmers were so damn hard up. By the time us kids got a hold of one of them inner tubes, there was more patches on it than Joseph's coat. The trick was to try and cut a couple straight strips between those patches.

Take it from me, just collecting some of the materials for our weapons of war often almost precipitated violence. Generally, I would sneak my mom's only good pair of scissors from the old Singer sewing machine to perform the operation that would be the envy of a brain surgeon. She would constantly remind me that if I took her good scissors "one more time," a brain surgeon was just what I was going to personally require. Was everybody's mother crazy when you "borrowed" their good scissors, or was my mom a special case? She didn't realize it was a jungle out there, and us kids had to be armed.

Anyway, along with that good red rubber, we needed pliable well-worn leather for a pouch. Tongues from old shoes were perfect. And that's another thing: if you cut out a tongue from shoes your dad or the hired man were still wearing, there was more hell to pay. Everybody was so damn touchy. String, however, was no problem. In those days, groceries weren't wrapped in Velcro, plastic, Glad, bad, and sad bags.

After the slingshot was made all you needed was a wagon load of small, round river stones, a few old tin cans—or better still, whisky bottles—and a handy fencepost or two. Hell, it was better than Nintendo, and you didn't need batteries.

In any case, the gopher didn't give a damn for perfect slingshots. Twenty-twos were a lot deadlier, but shells were expensive. In the end most gophers met their maker from poisoning and gopher traps. Lots of times the gopher would drag that trap a foot down his hole, and you had to pull him out, squeaking in terror till you banged him on the head. Then you'd spring open the trap, pick him up by the tail and fling him over your head with a snap. The gopher went flying, and you had the tail—which had come clean off the bone—left in your hand.

A trapped gopher went through hell, as some people never checked their traps for days on end. The lucky ones got trapped around the neck and died fast, but most got trapped by a front or hind leg.

Poisoning by strychnine was likely not a pleasant death either. One time I left a half-bucket of gopher poison near the barn and six of our pigs got into it. Before you knew it, a couple were laying on their sides, squealing and kicking and frothing at the mouth. Then two more went down. My dad was going to commit murder: mine. But first he hollered for Mom to mix a bucket of mustard and water. They poured that down the pigs' throats. Well, three of them died but three were saved; four, if you count me. Looking back, I don't think I ever saw Dad madder. It was a big loss; they were fine hogs. Actually, I think my mother saved my neck, and the best part was she ended up giving Dad hell for allowing a young kid like me to handle such deadly stuff. Way to go, Mom.

On rare occasions water was available and we drowned the gophers out. Sometimes it would take five or six buckets to fill up their hole, then you would see the water move, then bubbles, then the gopher would stick his head out, looking like a drowned rat. You clubbed him on the head, and another gopher soul went winging to that great gopher hole in the sky. (This was before the great hole in the ozone layer.) Then we'd strip off another wet gopher tail, sometimes two. That meant one more cent toward those CCM skates in the catalogue.

The gophers lost a thousand battles but they never really lost the war. A few still survive on the prairies, and I for one am glad. They paid their dues.

Joe's Cafe

Whenever our half-breed hired man got paid, he would take me—a kid of twelve—to Joe's Cafe and order coffee and two pieces of banana cream pie. God, I don't know what heaven's all about, but if they don't make banana cream pie, I say to hell with it. I'm not sure what made Joe's pies so damned good; those black bananas he used were eligible to vote, or at least past the age of majority. And the other ingredients were of unknown and mysterious origin. But man, was that pie delicious.

Joe was as mysterious as his pies. He was always pleasant and he lived alone, as did all the other Chinese cafe owners in those prairie towns. The rumour in Battleford was that Joe had a half-breed girlfriend from time to time from south of town.

Yes folks, kids of twelve know all about rumours, too. But it don't matter a whole hell of a lot one way or the other to Joe's bones resting back in China. Frankly, I hope the rumour was true. Canada was so damn racist back then to those hardworking, honest and independent people. I expect if things weren't so tough back in China, most of those folks would have gone back home.

I really want to say a word for all the other Joes who stuck it out in their lonely little cafes spread in almost every godforsaken, dying town on the prairies. What made them stay in those towns, where all you heard was the creaking signs of the John Deere and Imperial oil dealers? I want to ask all the Joes, "How come you came to the far edge of the world where the language was foreign, where you were tolerated only so long as you stayed in your place, and where you weren't even allowed to bring your wife or girlfriend, as every other damn immigrant was?" I want to ask, "How did you people stay so placid and law-abiding?"

I suppose independence had a lot to do with it, and a dream of being their own boss. Maybe conditions back home were so bad those solitary Chinese men were willing to work all hours in that killer prairie climate, living above, behind or beside their tiny cafes.

On the outside, they always seemed pleasant and cheerful— that must have something to do with Eastern philosophy. I'm sure if those folks had been Moslems, Jews, or even good Christians they would have found it a lot rougher in those small communities. Still, when you are the only one of your kind in a small town, and when your customs and language are totally foreign, you would probably have your work cut out for you no matter where you lit.

It's not that prairie people were more racist than the rest of Canada. In most respects they were quite the opposite. Prairie people, like people anywhere the climate is tough, had a greater degree of neighbourly and community spirit than you found elsewhere in the country. And that remains true today.

In those days my dad used to sell bulk milk to the four cafes in North Battleford, three of which were Chinese-owned and operated. Sometimes I would accompany him as he carried the milk cans into those kitchens. The Chinese cook would greet us with a huge smile and a meat cleaver. I stayed awful close to my dad 'cause I'd heard plenty of nasty nursery rhymes and fairy tales regarding the Chinese, especially Chinese carrying meat cleavers. I figured I had a good chance of becoming the main course in that day's dinner.

My dad would write the amount of milk he had delivered on the back of a calendar that hung in those kitchens, and once a month he'd tally up the amount. He was always paid in cash. This process went on for twenty or thirty years. He was paid every nickel he was owed, and never was there a word as to the quality or cost.

Chinese pioneers seemed to regard work as a privilege, and for the most part, they sure the hell weren't afraid of it. On the railroads, on the green chains, on the truck farms, in laundries and corner stores across Canada, they toiled away. They have made one hell of a contribution to the building of this nation and have certainly paid their dues.

To all the Joe's Cafes still left on the prairies: Hang in there! Some kid may still remember the banana cream pies.

Old Wives' Tales

Us kids stood in the water up to our knees in the rapids, at six-foot intervals, clean across the Battle River. We were petrified, but the local constable told us to stand there in case the body came up out of the water at the bend fifty yards upstream.

We had all seen plenty of dead animals. Farm kids see a lot of animals killed to eat or to sell, but a dead human body? The thought had us terror-stricken. Still, in those times, when a policeman said something, you never questioned it. Certainly ten-year-olds didn't.

I still remember a goldeneye swimming right into the shallow water near the bank, attracted by the light from one of several bonfires that had been set along the beach. The fires provided light for the police, who were working a small punt with grapple hooks in the deep water at the curve of the river.

The goldeneye was a good-sized fish, and I nailed it with a lucky first crack from a two-pound rock. I immediately felt guilty, but it wasn't just the guilt that comes from being Catholic, where guilt is the flagpole and mainstay of the creed. No, this was different. Somebody had drowned a few hours before, the body was still in the river a few yards away, and there I was doing something as frivolous as killing a goldeneye. It didn't seem very damn respectful.

In those days a death meant dark clothes for the women and black armbands for the men. These were worn for six months to a year or two after the funeral of a family member or friend.

I laid that fish on the bank, gave it a couple more whacks on the head and resumed my place in the rapids. Car headlights were visible bumping up and down the hill to the highway. Later in the night, the RCMP from North Battleford arrived with another boat and two divers. Several times us kids thought we saw something in that shallow water, but it was only our imaginations fuelled by the ever-moving shadows from the flickering bonfires. We breathed a sigh of relief when someone came up with the bright idea of stringing an old tennis net, brought out from Battleford, across the rapids where we had been standing.

It was just after midnight. Mist was hanging over the river as the land cooled. I picked up the goldeneye, put a stick through its gills and, with my brothers and sisters, walked up the hill to the house.

The body was recovered with a grapple hook at three-forty and put in the back of a Model A pickup.

Looking back, it was a dumb idea to put young kids through that trauma. The water being so shallow, a body could not have floated past in any event.

During summer holidays us kids would stay for hours in that piss-warm river, watching the swallows skimming the water and disappearing into their neat, round holes in the clay banks. Often, too, it was picnic time on the riverbank, and my mother would bring down sandwiches and, on very rare occasions when we could afford it, store-bought buns and wieners. Then we would light a small fire and have a wiener roast. Just us, and several million mosquitoes.

A handyman half-breed friend and his family used to pitch

their old canvas teepee at that picnic site for several weeks each summer. He made a few bucks doing the odd renovation or repair to our house or outbuildings. My father, with his booming voice, was wanted throughout the district to chair CCF meetings, to toast brides and sing at church or what have you. But when it came to fixing anything he was a total abject flop. Consequently my mother eagerly anticipated those visits from our half-breed friend.

It was one of those burning afternoons, not a breeze to stir a single leaf. Us kids were in the water, two hundred yards up from the deep hole where the river curled ninety degrees, just before the rapids. The deep hole was strictly out of bounds to us kids. We were told it was bottomless, with whirlpools that would drag you under like a stone and hold you there forever. In fact, the water at that spot was probably seven, maybe eight feet at the deepest. Then again, to a four-foot kid, eight feet of water was pretty awesome.

Somehow the three hired men from the neighbouring farm got into the deep water that afternoon without us kids noticing. They were skinny-dipping and having a hell of a good time and not hurting anyone. They were mostly underwater anyway, and we couldn't see anything even if we knew they were there.

But our half-breed handyman thought these men might be in the nude, and he didn't like it. You see he was Christian, and all good Christians (and especially Catholics) believe they aren't even born in the nude. Nope, they come out with clothes on, sometimes even with brass buttons and cowboy boots. I recall being told by the nuns never to sleep without clothes, as you gotta have clothes to get to heaven. That's just in case you died during the night.

So our handyman was only doing what was normal. He hollered at those men and gave them holy hell for not having respect for his wife or us kids. The three immediately started to panic and clear out. I am quite sure they had not even noticed us kids lying in the river upstream.

Anyway, they scrambled up the bank and grabbed some

clothes. That's when they noticed that one guy was missing. Well, the problem became all the more serious on account of a well-known old wives' tale. You see, it was written in stone in those days that a drowning person will grab any rescuer in a death grip, thereby dooming both to a watery grave. Us kids heard that tale a thousand times and thought it had to be true.

But the adults also believed in the tale. Even with bubbles rising to the surface just a few feet offshore, not one of the men on shore dove in to save that drowning man. Our handyman was urging the two to jump in, yelling, "He's right there!", "He's right there, God damn it." Still, they did nothing. The handy man himself made a small effort at a rescue, jumping into the water in his bib overalls, but he only got up to his waist. He was a good ten feet from where the bubbles were still rising. Yes, our handyman and those other two stood there petrified, totally immobilized with fear, as that poor bastard drowned in the curve of the river just feet away. I never knew someone could die so silently, so quickly.

One other fairy tale blown to hell that day was, "A drowning person always comes up three times."

The autopsy later said it was a simple case of drowning. I think it should have read, "Cause of death: modesty, religious phobia and old wives' tales."

My Aunt Pat

If a Liberal or Conservative ever got upwind of my aunt Pat, you had fire on the water. She had no time or truck with those phoney, arrogant, self-serving pompous bastards. Pat lived and died a CCFer and was never hesitant to let all and sundry know what she thought of the old-line parties on the prairies, whose members' only objectives were, she said, to get reelected to feather their own nests.

Politics to Pat was meant for the help and betterment of the poor farmers and workers in those depression years. And the CCF was the only party with any platform or policy that empathized with the poor people. Convincing the average voter, however, was another matter. In those days all the Catholics (there were many) were told by their parish priests that to vote anything other than Liberal was close to treason and might even lead to excommunication. So the poor, dumb, religious farmers did as they were told, and the fat Liberals and priests lived almost forever and ever.

Now Pat was also Catholic but she sure the hell never fit the "dumb farmer" role. And nobody, especially no damn parish priest, was going to tell her how to vote, period.

Pat was married in 1920 to August Gerster, a good-natured Danish immigrant who had a homestead a couple of miles south of Borden. August was active in the Saskatchewan Wheat Pool, the school board and the Borden Grazing Co-op. They had four children. The two younger ones, twin girls, died in a tragic accident along with their father in 1947. Pat herself was very severely injured in the same accident and lay in a coma for several days.

That traumatic event would have been enough to flatten the average person. Well, we ain't dealin' here with your average person; we are dealin' with my aunt Pat. With her son Gilmour's help, Pat was able to continue farming. After some time, the old spark returned. She remarked to me, "I ain't near as pretty as I used to be, but I'm still gonna give them Liberals hell." The "pretty" comment was in reference to the facial reconstruction job and the plate she carried in her skull from the accident. To me and everyone else in Borden she looked just fine.

My aunt Pat typified a lot of those early prairie women: they had guts and they had courage. I hope they haven't all gone the way of the buffalo. I would like to believe Pat is still giving it to the Liberals up yonder, but I don't think the Liberals are in the same place.

Poison Shmoizen

Once kids are past the caterpillar-, crap-, and mud-eatin' stage, they often become paranoid about food that is even slightly strange. It's "poison," they say. As kids on the farm we were just the same.

Having grown up on a poverty-striken prairie farm during the depression, we shouldn't have been all that damn touchy about dying of food poisoning. We had one hell of a lot better chance of disappearing down one of them abandoned wells scattered around the place, or dying under a horse or our Model A Ford pickup truck on any Saturday night. But it was strange food we feared more than anything.

Maybe what put us off was reading about that stuff old Socrates drank, just to show them other fellows he was serious. Before I read about old Soc, I thought hemlock was a west coast wood that didn't burn so good.

My mother, on the other hand, didn't have the slightest fear of strange food. Perhaps it was because she was Swiss, and the Swiss don't have anywhere near the fear of dying us Canadians do. Mother would "taste," or eat anything that wasn't actually moving, and even some things that were. She died in her eighties, and it wasn't from food poisoning.

Every substance known to mankind that had, over the many years of its life, lost its label or instructions for use, was quickly and easily identified by my mother's foolproof method of tasting. Yep, whether it came in a can or a bottle, whether it looked like something you were supposed to put in the transmission of your truck or ram down the throat of a sick cow, my mother "tasted" it all. Us kids would watch, waiting for her to drop dead on the spot.

"Old girl," my dad would say, "you're gonna kill yourself one of these days." Little did he realize that by calling her an "old girl," he was in far greater peril of dying than she was.

"Oh, shurrup!" was her usual reply, which I think was Swiss Canadian for, "Keep your trap shut."

Now, you take any food or fruit, canned or otherwise, that had gone moldy—and I mean so moldy that us kids knew it would kill you instantly, even if you just sat next to it—why, my mom would just scrape or spoon a little mold off the top and pronounce it "good as new." Being only half-Swiss, we were generally only half-convinced.

One thing I do know for certain is that my mother must have discovered penicillin long before those turkeys came up with the bread mold idea. I'll never forget some of our home-canned fruit that hadn't sealed properly in those old glass jars with rubber rings. It was carpeted in a fuzzy fur, like something out of a monster movie. I'm sure the average modern woman would have fainted dead away, or at least gotten the vapours at the sight of that stuff. But not my mom. She would just be singing something in Swiss, spoon off a little of that hairy monster, dump the rest in a pan and boil it down for dinner.

Most of the time, we really didn't know what went on out in that kitchen; in that era, a kid never asked too many questions. Still, through it all, my mom raised eight kids and none of us ever died of "poison." Of course maybe that's because we're half-Swiss.

With This Ring

My uncle Garnet was great at raising kids and great at public speaking, but as far as farmin' or fixin' went, he was, like my dad, no great shakes. To be fair, Picasso probably couldn't fix a combine either. Not everyone can be farmers and fixers. Still, my uncle was a great guy, huge in stature but gentle as a pussycat and totally committed to the socialist philosophy and the betterment of fellow beings.

Uncle Garnet lived on a quarter section homestead in a log house near the village of Delmas, a few miles west of Battleford. The family was bare-bones poor, but always had enough to eat and always seemed happy. For some strange reason they regarded us as the rich cousins from Battleford. Things being relative, I suppose folks living in log houses would regard anyone living in a frame house (as we did) as wealthy. Uncle Garnet, in his capacity as reeve, councillor and school board trustee, made frequent trips to meetings in Battleford and would often camp overnight at our dairy farm on the way home.

It was on such a trip that I heard him tell my dad—over the course of three or four pipes of tobacco—about the ring. His wife Mary, a perpetually smiling, optimistic woman, carried most of the load on that homestead, as did most pioneer women of those times. Besides making all the family clothes, canning, cooking and cleaning—all without running water or electricity—they also did all kinds of farmyard chores. There should be statues all over the prairies to those Saskatchewan pioneer women.

Now the one and only possession of value Mary had was a plain gold wedding band. You can imagine the trauma when one day she noticed the ring gone. She never ever took the ring off to wash dishes or whatever, so she knew she hadn't casually put it away for safekeeping. For weeks and months they searched without success for that ring. The solitary article she owned of worth and sentimentality had vanished.

Then my uncle Garnet had a dream in which he was walking with Mary in the farmyard. Suddenly she started falling into one of their abandoned wells—those death traps that covered so many prairie farms. He grabbed her hand just as she was slipping down, but he couldn't hold her.

He woke up from that nightmare in a cold sweat. When he opened his hand, he had her ring. To the day he died, he never ever was able to figure how it happened.

Go for the Horses

Sometimes after waking to the faint odour of smoke from a crackling wood fire in the kitchen stove downstairs, or to the ominous sounds of my mother banging pots while singing in Swiss, I used to stretch languorously farther under my patchwork quilt and pretend I hadn't heard her. The acoustics in that old clapboard house weren't too good, and I hoped she would get so busy down there she would plumb forget me. Or I hoped for the miracle of miracles, that our bloody horses would come home by themselves.

Most of the other farmers had horses waiting at the barn door at dawn to be fed and harnessed. Ours were a different breed. Pulling a disc or a set of harrows around a hot dusty field all day was not exactly their idea of a good time. Consequently they had to be fetched, surrounded, outflanked, coaxed and coerced into the barn. Even with all available hands waving hats and switches and my father hollering loud enough for our neighbours (at a half-mile) to hear quite clearly, the black horse we called Nigger would summon up a magnificent burst of speed and breach our line with snorts and farts. With mane and tail flying, he would gallop down to the river.

As soon as one horse had escaped, the other horses—as well as my father—would become frantic. Father would be shouting, "Whoa, whoa, you dirty black son of a bitch." The horses would charge our line, wheel and turn at the last second, till one of us eventually took a step the wrong way, and one by one they would slip through. The only exception was the old mare Jessie, who was twenty-four years old and past such foolishness. At this stage I used to bridle her up and gallop off in hot pursuit to start the whole process over again. My father said horses were like apples and the black devil was spoiling all the rest.

Back in my bedroom the window was open and a little breeze was blowing the sun-faded chintz curtains. Outside a meadowlark was going, "Phleet, phleet, phleet, phleeta leeta leet." In the distance the whistle of a freight train rose and fell with the wind. All the while noises from the kitchen were getting louder.

The air had a lingering smell of Vicks VapoRub, administered the night before—over protests from each of us kids—to nose and chest, cold or not. My mother said it was good for us, and we usually got what was good for us.

In bed I was thinking of that lucky bugger of a sister of mine who broke her collarbone. She didn't have to go to school for two whole weeks. I racked my head to think of something I could catch or break, so long as it didn't hurt too much.

"You better get up before Daddy gets back from milking." The words of doom rang up those stairs.

The sun was climbing and it looked like the day was going to be a scorcher. I crawled out of bed and slipped into a faded pair of jeans. I don't mean the kind you buy faded right from the store, for which you pay an extra twenty dollars for having some other guy make them look old, and therefore make you look poor. Nosirree, these jeans were faded the old-fashioned way, by washing them three hundred times, usually by hand, with strong lye soap. Hell, in those days we were too damn dumb to know that it was "in" to be poor.

I put on a new shirt my mother had made, which I had

placed under my pillow the night before, just in case my brother got any funny ideas. While I trusted my brother as much as possible, I didn't plan to leave no brand-new shirt just laying out in plain sight. I was having some trouble finding my socks—they not being under the bed and all—so I called down to my mother. "Open your eyes," she replied. It seemed like a rather silly suggestion at that hour of the morning.

My mother's voice had the tone of a woman working with wet wood, so I did not persist in looking for the socks. I pulled a pair of ratty running shoes over bare feet and carefully made my way down to the kitchen.

"Daddy wants you to go for the horses," my mother said, without turning from the stove. "You can have breakfast when you get back." It sounded like my father was in for a hot time for not laying in a store of dry wood "like the neighbours always do."

The sun was already blazing when I walked down the warped planks of our creaking front steps. All those prairie houses were dying for a little paint, but who in the hell could afford it? I rounded the corner of the house and headed for the pasture. It was on the other side of the railway tracks, which cut our property in two.

I unlocked the big steel gate, and after a hurried look to see that no one in the yard was looking, I rode it across the road, hopping off just before it slammed the other side with a kind of a wild goose creak.

At the railroad I put my ear to the rail; the steel was still cool. I couldn't hear anything, so I sauntered to the highway which ran parallel with the tracks. Picking up half a dozen round rocks off the road, I crept stealthily down the bank and peered into a large drainage culvert to see if there were any gophers inside. There were none, and lucky for them too.

I walked along the ditch, looking for beer bottles. The call of the neighbours' rooster came over the field. For some reason, it couldn't crow as well as our own. By now the sun was climbing fast and meadowlarks were everywhere. I picked up a beer bottle with a chipped top and looked right at the sun through the dark-coloured glass. It made the rest of the sky look dark and ominous, so I threw it at a fencepost.

The pasture gate was made of barbed wire and willow pickets, with two wire loops on the gatepost to hold the gate tight. Our hired man was the strongest man in the world and he could hold the gate tight with one hand and slip the wire over that gate picket with the other hand easy as pie. I could never figure why those damn gates had to be so tight. The only way I could even come close to opening the gate was if I held the gate picket with one arm, hooked my other arm around the fencepost and pulled with all my strength. I could just get the top loop slack but I needed a third hand to lift the top loop over the gate picket. I would have lifted the top loop with my teeth, but there was a barb in the loop at that critical point. So I gave up, found an old broken picket, and after several smashes, managed to knock that loop over the top. The gate went flying, damn near scratching me up in the process.

After dragging the gate clean out of the way so those bloody horses couldn't get their feet tangled up, I followed a well-worn cow path to the far end of the pasture where the horses were grazing. As I got closer and circled around, the black horse lifted his head, eyed me suspiciously and snorted. His nostrils flared. Once again, I knew me and my father had our work cut out for us.

A Hot Beef Sandwich

There's an old, faded brick building in south Battleford that was once a place of learning, at least for some folks. One of the bricks from that venerable building now sits on my desk with an inscription which reads, "BCI Fiftieth Reunion."

It's been fifty years since I attempted to get an education at the old Battleford Collegiate Institute. Few things have stuck with me through the years, unless you count the ability to sneak a smoke at recess without: (a) the principal catching you, or (b) a sparrow or a pigeon shitting on your head as you huddled close to the wall under the eaves which were covered with open-mouthed gargoyles and nesting birds.

The old collegiate has been replaced by one of them new-fangled, flat-roofed wood and glass jobs that will probably need major surgery within the first five years. Meanwhile, though, it looks good.

When I take a close look at my brick, and a good look in the mirror, I'm forced to concede that those fifty years were kinder to the brick. Thinking back to school days I recall two things: the school colours were purple and gold, and a Ukrainian teacher, Mr. Mkeechuck, who I am sure has long since gone to that great high school in the sky.

Mr. Mkeechuk was regarded by the school board, and all the other high school teachers, as the worst teacher who ever taught in Battleford, and possibly the worst in the whole of Saskatchewan. But us kids loved him. We could goof around as much as we liked in his class 'cause he was always reading either the *Saskatoon Star Phoenix* or the *Winnipeg Free Press*. We sure the hell had lots of fun, even though we all failed his class. He was always telling us what a lousy, poor-paying job teaching was and how he planned to get a real job soon—in the shipyards in Vancouver, where he could make some "real money, for a change."

One summer evening Mr. Mkeechuck met me and another high school student on the street in North Battleford. He asked us how we were doing and if we'd like him to buy us something to eat. Well, you know teenagers and seagulls seldom turn down anything to eat, especially if it's free, so we said, "Sure."

He took us to the Savoy Cafe and ordered three hot beef sandwiches. Layer upon layer of thinly-sliced roast beef piled on genuine store-bought white bread, smothered with rich brown gravy, with real ketchup right out of the bottle. God, I thought I'd died and gone to heaven.

A week later our favourite teacher disappeared. The rumour was that he got fired for lack of academic skills or standards of teaching. Us kids were glad, 'cause we knew he was headed for a Vancouver shipyard and some "real money."

Fifty years later I don't remember my other teachers' names, but I do remember Mr. Mkeechuck and my first ever hot beef sandwich.

Tapping Maples

When the warm spring winds hit the prairie, and slender stems start pushing through rotting snow, the sap is ready in Saskatchewan.

About a half mile from our house, on the river flat near the train bridge, stood a grove of some forty old Manitoba maples. This was my happy hunting ground for sap. After waiting what seemed a lifetime for Saturday to come around, I'd get up early, gulp my porridge and try to find a matching pair of gum boots (without too many holes). Then I'd tell my mother to find thirty or forty clean cans and I'd dash outside.

After rummaging around the shop I usually found a piece of galvanized tin that had fallen off the chicken house roof. I cut it up into two-inch squares with a pair of old, dull snips that dug into my hand and hurt my fingers. My dad said they needed sharpening, but the hired man said they were "no damn good."

I cut about thirty squares, then pounded them flat on the anvil, as the dull snips had turned up all the edges. Then, with the precision of a brain surgeon, I placed them one by one in the vice and hammered them into a ninety-degree angle, so each resembled a tiny trough. Next, I found a bucket that had been a milk pail in its prime, and dumped in the troughs. I also put in a hammer, some nails that I pulled out of the wall, some haywire and a brace and bit. The hired man said the bit was too big, but it was the only one we had.

Back in the house my mother had all the cans washed and ready. Looking back, I really don't know how she could find all those cans on such short notice. Peanut butter cans accounted for the largest group, followed by jam tins and honey and syrup cans.

After loading the tins into an apple box I placed it and the bucket of tools onto my sleigh and tied them with binder twine. Then, taking the dogs along just in case I ran into some dangerous wild animal, we all set off for the tall timbers. I crossed the ravine behind the house and plodded through the snow across the river flat. The dogs galloped ahead, stopping occasionally to sniff a rabbit track or see if I was still travelling in their general direction.

The maple grove lay at a bend in the river, and in summer a wagon trail passed right through it. The trail was used for hauling hay from a field on the other side.

When I reached the first large tree, I took out the brace and bit and drilled an inch-deep hole into the trunk, about two feet above the ground. The area around the hole became damp immediately. Then I drove a metal spout an inch below the hole—but not too deep—so the sap wouldn't run below the spout. Next, I drove in a small nail two inches directly above the spout. I also drove a nail through each side of a peanut butter can. After looping a piece of haywire through the holes in the can, I hung the can over the nail.

In no time at all, I had several trees tapped. The minute variations of the sap going plink, plink, plunk on the can bottoms was the finest symphony I ever heard.

The Mortgage Company

"**W**e can't pay the mortgage, we can't pay the interest, the mortgage company is gonna foreclose."

Mortgages hung like a blanket over those dirt-poor depression-era farmers. Mortgages seeped into every discussion, no matter what the original topic.

The mortgage, the interest. "They say we have to pay the interest this year, or else." It's all people talked about.

"Let them have the damn schtoopid farm," my mother exploded one day.

"They don't want the farm, old girl, they want the money," my father replied.

It was the thirties. Our sun-blackened fields were barren—again. The only thing that survived in the drifting soil was Russian thistle. God imposed gophers, rust, hail, hoppers, drought and the Russian thistle on the farmer, but did he have to include the mortgage company too?

Our dairy farm was three miles west of old Battleford on the Lloydminster--Edmonton highway. We sold the milk to the towns of Battleford—Old Town and North Town, as we called them in those days. Some of the wheat farm folks were under the illusion that dairy farming was a profitable enterprise because we sold something every day, as opposed to three times a year. But Lord knows, an illusion was all it was.

Now, cows have two main purposes in life: eating and crapping. Sometimes they'll produce milk, too. Crapping, though, forever remains their strong suit, and shovelling shit will forever be the byword of the dairy farmer. Ever and ever, amen.

Feeding was the big rub in those days. How in hell do you feed forty cows, twenty young stock and eight horses with no crop? Simple, said wheat farmers, you sell the milk and buy the feed. The fact that it cost more to buy the feed than we got for the milk never seemed to influence them or their "rich dairy farmer" illusions.

How we really survived was very simple. We lost a little money on every quart of milk we sold but made it up on the volume. That little-known secret was also discovered by my wheat-farming uncles who, in the latter stages, took over our dairy farm to make their pile.

Cows, milk and crap notwithstanding, the king of topics bandied about remained the damn mortgage and the interest. God, it used to get boring and depressing. The way I figured it, money was only paper with printing, so all they needed to do was to print a few wagon loads of the stuff, give it to everybody who had a mortgage and—presto! Simplest thing in the world.

As the Dirty Thirties were about to become history, another word started popping up almost as frequently as the mortgage. The word all farmers spoke of, and usually with a kind of hallowed reverence, was the "coast."

The coast. Where was this magical place, where the water ran out of the rocks, winters were mild and everyone was rich? Could there really be a place where the crops didn't burn and where the thistles didn't roll up on the fences with the soil piling up behind, like snowdrifts in winter?

Could there be a land without vicious hailstorms, like the one that stripped all the leaves and bark from the maple windbreak that ran from our house to the highway? The windbreak had grown from six-inch seedlings my mother had dug from the banks of the Battle River and brought home, piled on top of me, in the baby carriage. My mother was always reminding me that those maples and I were the same age.

The same storm killed all our young chickens, who had mistakenly thought it would be safe to take refuge under those trees. I can still see their battered blue heads pounded into the mud. The storm broke all the windows on the north side of the house and then it went strangely silent. We emerged later to find hailstones the size of golf balls in little piles where they had been driven by the wind. Then the sun came out, and the land was steaming and peaceful, with a rainbow right down to the ground. Just like nothing had happened at all.

Was there a land where a sun-crazed farmer wouldn't walk out to his burnt field and put a .22 rifle to his head, so he'd never have to witness another crop start up green, then day after scorching day turn brown, then black? At the funeral, I heard someone say, "When I found him, his heels had dug into the soil six inches from kicking as he died." And funerals like that were not rare—it was a hell of a time. When somebody talks about the good old days, it might just be the blessing of a short memory.

Talk of the coast came up almost daily in my folks' conversation, and through the thin bedroom walls of our old wind-swept house another strange term, "BC," was plain to hear.

Then, suddenly, it happened. My oldest brother and sister moved to BC, followed the next year by my sister and brother-in-law from Saskatoon. Next spring, another brother and sister were lured by the letters home from BC, which spoke of plenty of work and flowers in February.

Originally there were eight in our family. Now we were down to five—Mom, Dad, my younger brother, my sister and myself. Things were moving fast. Families all over Saskatchewan were heading for the coast. Still, I was sure it was chiselled in stone somewhere that my folks would never leave the old homestead and their beloved Battle River.

The very next week, however, my wheat-farming uncles arrived and made a deal whereby they would take over the dairy—lock, stock and us three kids. And just like that, my folks were on their way to the Promised Land. They said they would send for us later. So much for stone-writing.

The Promised Land was on my mind too. Before long I was talking about the coast with Johnny, a half-breed hired man, or should I say boy—I was fifteen, he was sixteen—that worked at another uncle's dairy farm a few miles away. Johnny and I had chummed around on Sundays, shooting gophers or riding around on our bikes. At first our talk about leaving was flippant, but soon it got serious. Our number one priority was secrecy, as we knew if my uncles found out we had designs on the coast they would do everything possible to stop us.

We faced two major obstacles. The first was money, the second was transportation. The latter problem was solved almost instantly because we both had bicycles. Johnny had borrowed his, nearly new, from another hired man whom he planned to pay back later, wink, wink, nudge, nudge. The poor bugger is probably still waiting for his money.

My bike, like Joseph's coat of many colours, was made of pieces cannibalized from other ancient models. Although my four- or five-colour bike could be basically described as a single-speed CCM with coaster brakes, its tires were bald and a lot of the cords were showing. So we had transportation—hell, it was only fifteen hundred miles.

Now, for money. Johnny had twenty-seven dollars. I borrowed five from our hired man, boosting my own total to twelve dollars. By our standards, we had a small fortune.

The days were dragging, and Johnny finally told my uncle he was leaving. My uncle was madder than hell, threw down the last two dollars of Johnny's pay, said we wouldn't make the first twenty miles and headed for the barn. The uncles with whom I was living were both away when I lit out, so that saved another scene.

We had front baskets and back carriers on our bikes to carry our blankets (no sleeping bags, just heavy old blankets), a couple of sandwiches, a bicycle pump and a tire repair kit for my bald old tires.

My aunt came out to see us off. She still thought we were kidding, but my younger brother and sister, John and Betty, sure the hell looked forlorn. How could I abandon them? It wasn't all that easy. I suppose it was sort of like survival of the fittest, or at least the oldest.

It was the summer of '41, and the time was nine-thirty in the morning. We waved good-bye and started out for Battleford, which was three miles away by gravel road. The plan was to go south from Battleford to Wilkie, pick up another co-conspirator and continue our journey west.

It was a hot day, and soon after heading south from Battleford—with Bishop's flour mill (the tallest structure in town) gradually shrinking in the distance—the good gravel road petered out. From then on we were running through three inches of sand ground to a fine consistency over the decades by thousands of iron-tired wagon wheels.

The theory of our route, plus our mode of transportation, was supposed to be foolproof. Instead, it was damn tough going. What I needed was a Harley, not a broken-down one-speed bike. Johnny was a bit ahead and he was sweating too. We stepped off our bikes to push them up a hill when a truck dragging a tail of dust for half a mile roared up. Hell, it was Murphy's old International from the lumberyard in town, and young Bill was driving. He stopped.

"Where the hell are you guys going?" he asked.

"Goin' to the coast."

"You gotta be kidding."

"Where you going?" we asked.

"I got a couple tons of coal to take to the school about eight miles up the road." Before you knew it, we had loaded our bikes on the bags of coal and climbed into the cab. Man, it was good to be riding with the windows down. When we hit that little country school, we helped Bill unload the coal and said goodbye. He went north and we headed south. The road got a little easier after our rest, if you can call unloading coal on a hot summer's day a rest, but that's how it is when you're young with energy to burn.

At about nine-thirty that night we arrived at the large and prosperous farm where we were to pick up our third musketeer. It had to be prosperous—the colour of the paint was still distinguishable on most of the buildings. Shortly after we arrived our man informed us he would be unable to leave. The old folks he worked for would be really stuck for harvest without him. So we scrapped plan A and referred to the owner's manual.

After realizing we weren't going to hijack their hired man, the farmers were real friendly. They fed us and said we could sleep in the hayloft, so long as we didn't smoke. Smoke? Hell, only millionaires could afford to smoke in those days. Also, it was fairly common for farmers to offer their barns for sleeping and the code of "No Smoking" was universally accepted.

Sleeping in hay is a treat; everyone should have the privilege of doing it sometime. Hay beats hell out of waterbeds, air mattresses and even them new-fangled posturepedic beds. It smells a lot better, too. One other advantage of sleeping in a loft: you don't need an alarm clock, the swallows get you up at four-thirty sharp.

Next morning the farmer's wife gave us a huge breakfast, made us two bags of sandwiches and wished us good luck and God speed. We were on the road before seven o'clock. The meadowlarks were all on pitch and the gophers were skittering across the dusty road. We knew it was gonna be a hot day. A couple of miles along the road, I got a flat tire. It was the first, but it sure the hell wasn't the last. By the time we reached the Alberta border late that evening I had had four flats, all on that bald front tire.

We slept out in the open that second night, but first we pedalled around the little village of Provost and out to a small lake a couple of miles away for a swim. Like I say, when you're young, you're crazy.

Next morning, after a doughnut and coffee, we set out in a light rainstorm. Those lucky Albertans. I knew they had oil, but rain too!

Now mention the word gumbo to folks on the coast and they think it's something to eat. But it ain't. Gumbo is mud. And gumbo mud isn't something to ride a bicycle on after a rainstorm. We rode into that stuff maybe a hundred yards, till our wheels jammed tight. We tried cleaning the wheels with a stick and got another fifty yards, then they jammed tight again. This we did again and again and again. When we got off to push the bikes, that crud built up under our boots like snowshoes. We made maybe a half-mile in two hours. There were still over thirteen hundred miles between us and the coast. Finally, we had to push our bikes along the fence line beside the road, where the grass covered the clay. A couple of miles farther on the road was dry and we got mobile again.

No sooner had we passed the mud, when—pop!—my front tire blew. This time it wasn't any little stone bruise. The whole sidewall gave out near the rim, exposing the wire bead. I began invoking the Lord's name in vain. But after contemplating a twenty-mile walk to the next town with a flat wheel, I began thinking I should have gone to confession more and that on the few times I did go I should have told that senile old priest the truth. Now God was getting me back.

I laid the bike down on the road. As I straightened up, something red caught my eye in the ditch. Lying in the tall weeds was a near-new bicycle! And the wheels were the same size as mine! God didn't hate me after all.

I hollered to Johnny. We thought first of taking the whole bike, but changing the carrier and front basket would have taken too long, so a front wheel swap was the logical thing to do. Frantic, we got out the crescent wrench and pliers, swapped the wheels, and were just about finished when along came three kids on bikes. We figured, "Tonight it's gonna be the jailhouse for sure."

The kids stopped and looked at the new bike, which now

had my old wheel. "There's that rich Sutter kid's bike," said one of them, after a long silence. "He's always throwing it in the ditch." Then they rode off. I have often wondered what the kid thought when he found that old flat wheel on his bike. Those kids said he was rich, so me and Robin Hood have something in common—the only difference is, I stole from the rich and kept it.

So Johnny and I eluded the prison bars and were heading for the coast with at least one good tire. Onward and westward, no more flat tires, no more gumbo. The gods were looking kinder upon us. We spent that evening at a small farm just outside of Camrose. Our money was holding, but just. In those times, fifty bucks would take you halfway around the world.

The fifth night we hit Calgary, the biggest city in the world. We went into a lane to sleep and crawled under some cardboard packing cases. Later I found a huge piano crate lined with shavings, crawled inside and fell asleep.

By this time we figured bicycling through the Rockies might not be all that much fun. Next morning, we had coffee and doughnuts in a small cafe and asked the waitress if she knew anyone who wanted to buy a couple of bikes. She went into the back a minute, reappeared and said, "Maybe. How much?" Johnny said fifteen dollars and I said five dollars. We sold both bikes for twenty dollars and then went to the post office and mailed our blankets and stuff General Delivery to Vancouver. We were free!

After breakfast we hitchhiked out of Calgary. We got a lift from a farmer in an old pickup truck to just a few miles outside of Banff. We stayed one more night in a hayloft, milked a couple of cows and were back on the road by eight the next morning. Hitching was bad, but we got two more short lifts just out of Banff.

We were near a rail crossing somewhere up in that country when a west-bound freight train started moving. We'd never jumped a freight before, but we said, "What the hell," and ran for it. I grabbed a ladder at the back end of a boxcar and hung on. I learned later that the back ladder is the wrong one to grab, 'cause if you miss you fall between the cars. Anyway, I got on. But I couldn't see if Johnny did or not. Next stop I jumped off and found him in an open box car, all settled in like he owned the damn thing, along with four other hoboes who were also heading for the Promised Land.

Those seasoned hoboes told us of the towns with the bad railroad bulls, plus the danger of suffocation riding behind a steam engine through the numerous tunnels ahead. They sure scared the hell out of us, but after surviving the first couple of tunnels filled with coal smoke, steam and cinders, we knew we could make it.

That evening the train stopped for water. We jumped out and spotted a flatcar carrying a highway road grader. We climbed up, and damned if the cab on that grader wasn't open, so we scrambled in. It was great—glass all around to keep out the smoke and cinders. As the night drew on we started playing with the headlights on the machine. Minutes later the brakeman came walking over the top of the cars thinking he had a fire on board. He gave us hell but said we could stay, as long as we left those damn lights alone. We vowed we would never touch them again, and he left.

About this time we were hungry, and when the train pulled into Revelstoke we asked the brakeman how long it would stay. "A couple of hours," he said.

We ran to a cafe by the rail station and ordered clam chowder and toast. But just as the waitress brought the soup, the freight pulled out. That bastard had lied to us.

After our meal, we went to the station and discovered that the next freight wouldn't go through till late the following day. We checked the passenger fare. By pooling the last of our money, we could just make it to Port Coquitlam.

An hour later we were on the passenger train. God, we felt like kings, sitting on padded seats and looking out through side windows. No smoke or cinders for us; this was how the rich folks lived.

From the Coquitlam train station, we hitched a ride to New Westminster. It was about nine-thirty at night and the lights were just coming on over the new Pattullo Bridge. What a fabulous sight for a couple of prairie kids!

We asked a fella what river that was, and he said, "the Fraser." So that was the mighty Fraser we had heard so much about in school. It sure was a lot bigger than the Battle River back home, bigger even than the Saskatchewan, and a hell of a lot dirtier too.

We had fifteen cents left, so we went to a cafe and ordered two glasses of milk. The manager asked us if we wanted anything to eat but we said no. He went to the kitchen and came back with two beef sandwiches and placed them on the counter. We told him we didn't have any money.

"Forget it," he said. We were damn near starving, but didn't think it was that obvious. Our luck was still holding.

We were now just a dozen miles from our destination, which was a huge dairy farm in the Mud Bay area near White Rock. Yes, my parents were back in the lifestyle they knew and loved best—managing a huge dairy farm for a wealthy absentee owner. We walked the streets of New Westminster all that night, and when daylight came we walked over the Pattullo Bridge. A salesman heading for the US border dropped us off in Cloverdale, a pretty little farm town with flowers everywhere. What a contrast to the brown hills back home.

One more small ride and we walked the last mile along the King George Highway to the dairy, situated on the flats between the Serpentine and Nickomeckel Rivers. The clover was waist-high in the ditches. Everything was green.

By now I was pretty damn worried. My folks didn't know I was coming, and they may have expected me to stay put in Saskatchewan to help with the work back there. But there was no turning back.

We walked down the driveway to the huge shake-roofed barn. Beside the barn a pipe in the ground was running a full stream of cold water. Just a pipe in the ground—no pump, no shut-off valve. How was this possible? We learned later it was an artesian well. No wonder people left the dry lands of Saskatchewan, when in BC you could just stick a pipe in the ground and the water ran forever. Incredible.

We walked into the barn. It was milking time. My mother saw us first.

"Daddy, Daddy," she shouted, running up to us. "My God, it's the boys."

What a welcome! My dad shook our hands and my mom rushed to the house and threw together the biggest meal in the shortest time in recorded history. Nobody ever got past my mother without getting fed—whether you needed it or not—and man, we sure needed it. Later, we had a shower with real warm, soft, running water.

Before we hit the sack, my dad said "Did you really come out by bicycle?"

"Yep, clean across the mountains," we said, lying just a little.

"I'm sure glad to see you boys," he said. "We need some help for hayin'."

III.

Cariboo / Interior / Okanagan

Church Parade

Two things bore the ass off me. The first is listening to some army idiot hollering orders as you go through mindless robotic drills on a parade square; the second is listening to some church idiot spouting interminable, boring sermons or passages from the pulpit. When I was a kid and Catholic, I was forced to endure the latter. When I got into the army, I had to put up with drill parade plus church parade. So much for progress and enlightenment.

For part of the time I was in the army I was stationed in a small town in northern BC. On Sundays a couple buddies and I would often slip into the jack pine forest and go "big game hunting" for rabbits and squirrels with our .303 Lee Enfield rifles. The "big game," of course, was really to stay out of church. Those squirrels were in greater danger of falling out of a tree than being shot by one of us. Anyone who has tried to hit a fast-moving squirrel at a hundred feet with a large-calibre rifle will know what I mean. It was a good thing we weren't depending on them for food or their skins. However, we did knock down a lot of pinecones and branches, and a good time was had by all, including the squirrels.

But there is always a problem in paradise, and the problem I had was that one of my hunting partners, a fellow named Jensen, had the nasty habit of leaving his rifle cocked. He would see a rabbit or a squirrel and cock his rifle. Then the animal would move out of sight, and Jensen would carry on walking with that cocked rifle. When somebody does that time after time, you tend to get a little nervous, especially if the guy is walking behind you. After a half-dozen such performances, I figured I'm gonna start walkin' behind him and maybe try to educate him.

Now the Chinese say a picture is worth a thousand words. I tried a thousand words on Jensen and that didn't work. So I figured I would sort of, if not draw him a picture, at least get his attention so he might get the picture. It was a bit like the farmer who had a mule he couldn't train. One day, he heard about a mule-training expert in the next town, so he called him to come and train his mule. The expert shows up, looks at the mule, picks up a two-by-four and smacks that mule between the eyes. Well, when that mule fell down on his knees, the farmer said, "What the hell did you do that for, I thought you was gonna train him!" The expert said, "I'm going to. But first I had to get his attention."

So, one Sunday we were out hunting. A rabbit shows up, Jensen cocks his rifle, the rabbit disappears and Jensen carries on with the gun cocked, as per usual. Time for a lesson. I broke off a small branch as we were walking along and cleared it of all the smaller branches, leaving a two-inch stub near the end. I had a six-foot hook. Jensen was still walking along with that cocked rifle down low by his side. The other guy was behind me. I carefully reached forward and pulled his trigger with my hooked stick. KABOOM! Jensen went about four feet straight up, just like he was shot. Mad? He was so damn mad he wanted to shoot me right there. He might have too, but it was his last shell that had just discharged and I, for one, wasn't about to lend him more.

After that, Jensen didn't want to go big game hunting with me anymore. But I imagine whenever he hunts now, he watches that cocked rifle business.

Towing George's Logging Truck

L ac La Hache, or "Lake of the Hatchet" got its name, so the legend goes, when an Indian chopping a hole in the ice to water his horses slipped and let go of his hatchet. The hatchet went to the bottom and the lake has been known ever since for the incident.

Lac La Hache is a sleepy little village right on the lake in the rolling hills of Cariboo country, roughly three hundred miles north and east of Vancouver. Some time ago friends of ours moved up to Lac La Hache to run a small cafe, with gas pumps, in the centre of the village. Each time they returned to Vancouver they painted such a glowing picture of the place that my wife and I decided to go and have a look.

We thought the place was beautiful too. There were lots of loons on the lake and cattle dotted the hills. Shortly after we returned to Vancouver from our visit, the service station I operated in North Vancouver was sold. It seemed like a good time to give Lac La Hache a try.

Business-wise, the move was a disaster. But during the six months we stayed there we met more than our share of characters.

Take George, for instance. George was an independent, honest, rough-around-the-edges type of guy. He was another refugee from the dark confines of North Vancouver. "It just got too damn busy down there," he told me one day at Kelly's Chevron station, where I had set up my wheel alignment equipment.

George had one hell of a sense of humour, and he was an eternal optimist no matter how tough things were. George worked at several of the small, portable sawmills outside of town, but he never fancied working too long for somebody else, and soon he bought an ancient Chev truck, put a fifth wheel on her and bought a beat-up logging trailer from the Swede who owned the mill at Two Mile.

The first time George came through town he was on his way to the stud mill at the end of the lake with a load of logs. Kelly and I watched him grind past. All I can say is, George was lucky to be hauling at a time when those damn cops with their portable weigh scales weren't watching every road, 'cause he would have gone to jail. And I mean straight to jail, without passing Go.

To say George's truck was overloaded is an understatement. Hell, you could barely see the cab! The tires were so flat even the dogs took notice. As George later explained, "When you get paid by the board foot, you don't want to be makin' too many trips and wastin' fuel."

Kelly said, "You crazy bastard."

One morning Kelly and George arrived at my house in Kelly's old two-ton Dodge wrecking truck. Apparently George's logging truck had got into a soft spot and needed a little tow. They wanted some company.

We found the truck about six miles up an old logging trail, part-way around a slight curve. The cab was barely visible below a monster load of logs, and on one side the tandem wheels of the trailer were buried to the axles in mud. George had hit a boggy spot in the road. Kelly took one look and shook his head. "George, you gotta be kidding."

I said, "George, you're going to need a D-8 Cat to haul that thing out, and if you don't dump the logs first, your old Chev is gonna come out in two pieces."

But old George, who nothing seemed to faze, said to Kelly, "Let's just give it one little try. If nothing happens, I'll get a Cat."

Kelly was silent a long time and finally said, "Just to humour you, I'll try once. But I know it's stupid."

We put a choker around a jack pine in front of the wrecker and secured it to the front axle. Then we pulled out the winch line, hooked it onto the old Chev and took up the slack. George crawled into the cab, started her up and waved for Kelly to yard on the winch. There was a little tremble; Kelly gave the wrecker more gas. All of a sudden there was a hell of a crash. The roots on that jack pine had let go, and it had come down smack on top of the wrecker.

Kelly shut the Dodge off and crawled out through the broken glass and steam. The tree had knocked the radiator into the fan, buckled the hood and broke the windshield.

George thought the whole thing was hilarious. But Kelly, who was a big raw-boned Irish Catholic, didn't see the humour in the situation. I could see his blood pressure going up, so I decided, discretion being the better part of valour, not to join George in the hilarity. Besides, I was contemplating a six-mile walk home and didn't see anything so damn funny about that.

Kelly walked around the truck, and George walked around the truck, so what the hell, I walked around the truck, too. I had to admit it was a rather funny sight, still tied to the tree in front and tied to the logging truck behind. Releasing the winch line was no problem; but the front choker was wedged tight by the angle of the tree across the hood. Old George got out a chain saw he kept in the cab of his truck and started cutting the jack pine to pieces. We also had to cut off the fan belt 'cause the fan blades were jammed tight into the rad core.

George said, "Kelly, you're damn lucky I picked a nice wet spot to get stuck in so we got lots of water to fill that rad." Kelly was strangely silent as we filled every gas can, oil can and even

George's thermos and hard hat with that swamp water. Then we put as much water as possible in the rad, piled into the truck, and started for home. We had to stop every quarter of a mile or so to fill the rad, and by the time we got back, the old motor was so hot it was crackling. Kelly sold that old wrecker shortly afterwards.

As for George, I never did find out how he got his truck out. And Kelly never asked.

Cariboo Picnic

Sundays are for sleeping late. For lapsed Catholics, like myself, Sundays are also for feeling guilty. Thirty-five years since I've been to mass, and I still feel qualms about missing church. Amazing. It must be written in stone that in order to be a good Catholic you have to feel bad to feel good.

When we were in Lac La Hache, it was one of our kids' favourite tricks to pile into our bed on Sunday morning and ruin any chance for a sleep-in. This one Sunday morning my son Rod, three, and my daughter Tobie, eighteen months, came and started trampolining in bed. "Let's go for a picnic," hollered my wife Doreen. Under the circumstances it sounded like a good idea.

The morning was crisp and clear. I checked the oil and water in our '49 Ford and grabbed a handful of tools, just in case. Meanwhile, my wife made up a lunch, including juice for the kids and a dozen beer for us (in case the coffee ran out). After a hasty breakfast we piled into the car and headed past the village of Lac La Hache, made a left turn on the Timothy Lake road and said goodbye to civilization.

The countryside smelled of jack pine and dust from the

washboard gravel road, and the lupines and Indian paintbrush along the fenceline were in full bloom. As always, I thought of what the city folks were missing. Yet whenever I mentioned the Cariboo to my city friends, they said without fail, "That bloody country. Nothing but mud, dust, mosquitoes and blackflies."

Okay, so that part is true. What they forgot to mention, however, were the stone bruises on your car, the broken headlights and the winters that last forever. That's the real Cariboo. Still and all, you don't find Indian paintbrush, loons, whitefaces and cowboys on 18th Street in North Van, where I normally live.

We drove eight or ten miles until we were just past Timothy Lake. When the road petered out I continued on, straddling a ditch, to within twenty yards of an abandoned lodge whose porch was hanging cockeyed. The lodge was flanked by four cabins—or what used to be cabins. The walls were all that were left standing—the snow loads in that high country had proved too heavy over the years. The chinking had long since fallen away too, and chipmunks ran in and out between the logs.

The location, so near the lake and so beautiful, made me wonder why such a site would have been abandoned. We prowled through the old lodge, which smelled of pack rats and wood smoke. Its huge, natural stone fireplace was in good condition and still contained ashes from the last fire.

It wasn't long before the kids were hungry, so we laid out a blanket by the lake, unlimbered the cooler, cracked a beer and leaned back to look at the clear blue sky. It was an ideal time for contemplating the purpose of life and the wisdom of spending most of my time working in the city. We had just polished off the last of the sandwiches and were watching the kids chase frogs when Doreen remarked, "That sounded like thunder."

My friend George had told me it never rains this time of year, period. "Couldn't be thunder," I said. Well, the next thing we hear is the patter of raindrops. The rain was warm and soon the country started to smell fantastic. But when you have small kids, you kind of work on the conservative side, so I said, "Maybe we better pack up and drive back a few miles till this thing blows over."

As the rain picked up, we loaded the gear and two protesting frog hunters. I slid behind the wheel and turned the key. The motor turned over fine but refused to start. Now, Fords of those years were damn fine cars but notorious for bad fuel pumps. So I lifted the air filter off and pumped the accelerator pump a few times. Nothing.

No problem. I had my coveralls, tool kit and a spare fuel pump in the trunk. Ten, fifteen minutes' work and we'd be rolling. On with the coveralls, off with the fuel pump (which Ford had the foresight to make easily accessible, if not reliable). The rain was getting heavier by now and a little trickle ran down the ditch the car was straddling. I tried the starter once more. Still nothing.

Strange. There was a full tank of gas, a new fuel pump, and still no fuel. The little trickle under the car was getting larger. What I had straddled was no ordinary ditch but a dry creek bed; usually dry that is.

I checked underneath the car near the gas tank. There was a wet spot where the gas line went over the rear axle housing. So that's why the new fuel pump wasn't working. Air was getting into the gas line through a small hole. I got some friction tape to wrap the line, but first I had to pry the line away from the frame. After a couple pries with a long screwdriver, that bloody rusty old line broke clean off. Oh-oh.

I crawled out, covered with gasoline, mud and water. The little stream under the car resembled one of the larger tributaries of the Amazon and it threatened to float the old car clean out into the lake. Invoking Henry Ford's name in vain, I peered through the rear window. Doreen was knocking back a beer and playing patty-cake with the kids. Then and there, I contemplated a sex-change operation and was wondering to myself, "Do they really need a women's lib movement?"

Whoever said necessity is the mother of invention had it only half-right; desperation is the other half. And when you're facing a ten-mile walk in a rainstorm with two small kids, you get a little inventive. The problem was how to get gas from point A to point C, without going through B.

First thing I did was start looking for containers to hold gas. Normally in the boonies you're stumbling over empty oil cans, coffee cans, plastic jugs and you name it, left by hunters and fishermen. But at this location there wasn't even a garbage dump back of the old lodge. I always carry a couple of spare quarts of oil in the trunk, so I checked the oil, figuring to top it up and get a small gas can in the bargain. Wouldn't you know it, the oil was right up. So there I am, pouring a full quart of oil on the ground. I hate waste, but I hate walkin' more.

Luckily, the tank on that Ford had a bung in the bottom. In what was now a downpour, I crawled under the tank, carefully loosened the bung, and filled the can. I got a regular gas bath and lost two or three gallons before I was able to thread the bung back in tight. For sheer misery, it's hard to beat the feeling of gas running up your arm to the armpit.

The late Ma Murray, the famous editor of the Lillooet newspaper, used to say, "God willin' and the cricks don't rise." Well, God willin' or not, that crick under the car was risin' fast. Another few minutes and we wouldn't have got out.

Soaked through, I disconnected the flex line behind the fuel pump and placed it inside the can of gas. Then, I wired the can upright (remember, haywire is my middle name) and hoped I didn't get a fire from the open can of gas so near the spark plugs.

The car started right off, and after backing up a couple of hundred yards to a gravel spot, I was able to get off that damn stream. Other than having to make four more stops to fill the gas can and get the mandatory gasoline bath each time, the trip to town was uneventful. That is, if you don't count my wife complaining about the smell of gas in the car, or the kids wanting to know when we'd go on the next picnic.

Oh, George? You were wrong about the rain.

Rassling a Grizzly

The Twilight Lodge beer parlour, halfway up Lac La Hache Lake, was jammed with loggers, tourists and mill workers. It was a Friday, and payday.

There was only one table available, inhabited by a one-armed Indian who had a bandage on his head. I asked if he was alone, and he motioned with his one good arm to sit down. So I pulled out a chair, ordered two draft and took in the scene.

Outside a pair of loons were cruising a hundred yards offshore. The setting sun was still partly visible over the village and it turned the cabin windows across the lake to gold.

Perhaps it was because the jukebox was playing a hit tune by Jim Reeves called "He'll Have to Go," or maybe it was plain inquisitiveness, but I asked the fellow where he was from. He told me he lived on the Sugar Cane Reserve near Williams Lake, and that he went guiding for Buster Hamilton in Lac La Hache every hunting season.

I was curious as to why he had one arm with a hook and a bandage on his head but I figured I'd find out sooner or later. Besides, having had a few Indian friends and being brought up near several reserves in Saskatchewan, I knew that—unlike most white men—Indians don't feel they have to fill every available space with conversation.

I ordered us a couple more beers and this fella asked me what I did for a living. It turned out that Kelly's Chevron, where I was working as a mechanic, was where Buster did his business. The conversation going, I asked if he got any moose this year.

"Yeah," he answered, "that's why I got this bandage on my head." I asked if a moose had nailed him and he said no, the damage was done by a grizzly. "Me and that grizzly had a little rasslin' match," was how he put it.

I said, "From what I hear, guys don't live to tell about rassling grizzlies."

He told me how it happened.

"I was guiding up at Blackwater for a couple Americans from California. They got a big bull moose just before dark, and all we had time for was to bleed and gut it. We planned to go back to camp and bring the horses in the morning to pack it out. So we left, got to camp, made something to eat, had a few shots of bourbon and hit the sack."

"Bourbon?" I interrupted. "You like bourbon?"

"Hell no," he said. "Rye is bad enough."

He continued. "Well, next morning we took two pack-horses and got back to the moose about six. We wanted to pack him out before it got too hot. The horses were acting a little spooky when we got close to the moose, which was layin' just out of sight, behind a big deadfall. We got down off the horses and tied 'em to a jack pine. Usually we don't have to tie 'em up, but they were a little nervous and we didn't plan on walkin' back home. Besides, these were all young horses. I guess they could smell blood, so we didn't think too much about it.

"We climbed up over that deadfall, and there was a big grizzly on top of that moose. He wasn't fifty yards away. I never been that close to a grizzly before, a live one anyway. The wind was comin' our direction and he didn't see us right away. I told them two hunters, 'It's too dangerous to shoot from this close, so let's try and back out quietly.' We start movin' back, but one of those guys stepped on a dry branch, and the grizzly heard the snap.

"The bear stood up, fur bristling on his neck. He let out a low growl. I said, 'Let's get the hell out, that bear is the biggest I ever seen.' We had gotten back maybe a couple hundred feet more when that bear suddenly came over that deadfall like one of them fellas in the Olympics.

"We all had them new magnum rifles, but their magazines only hold three shells. The guide is always the last one to shoot, so one of them fellas fired off three rounds and took off. The bear kept chargin'. Then the other guy fired off three rounds and *he* takes off. But the bear wouldn't go down; he kept chargin' and was now just a few feet away. I got off two shots, and that grizzly was right on top of me. As I was falling backwards, I got off another shot, which blew off half his jaw. I still had the rifle, but he tore that away with his half jaw. Then I got my wooden arm in his mouth. He ripped that away too. Then he grabbed my head, and I could feel my skull crackin'. He kept skidding off my head with that half jaw. I think if I hadn't got him in the jaw with the last shot, he would have killed me.

"Meanwhile the hunters had reloaded, but they were afraid to shoot in case they hit me. Then the bear stood up one more time, one of the guys got him through the neck and he fell down. I crawled away, and they shot him in the head one more time."

"You must have caught a glimpse of the happy hunting ground," I said.

"Nope," he answered. "The worst part was the bear's breath." Turns out this adventure had only happened a couple days before, and the guide had just had his head stitched up at Williams Lake.

"Maybe you guys are pisspoor shots," I offered.

"I thought maybe those California guys were shooting wild," said the fella. "But later, when we skinned that bear out, it turns out every one of those shots should have stopped him. Once you wound a grizzly, and you're up close, you're in trouble. I shot a few grizzlies, but only from a long way off. If they can't smell or see you, they don't know where to charge."

I was thinking maybe this guide was a bit of a bullshitter, but just then he rolled up his sleeve and showed me his wooden arm with the hook. Huge teeth marks scarred the wood. "You gonna quit guiding now?" I asked, ordering another couple of beer.

"No," he replied, "next week Buster wants me to take out a couple rich guys from New York."

One for the Road in Williams Lake

Cisco Charlie, ramrod straight and pushing seventy, brought back all my childhood recollections of prairie Indians. With a beat-up, black ten-gallon hat I'm sure he wore to bed, silver sideburns making his wind-tanned face even darker, and sharp, proud features, he looked ready to mount a pinto bareback and trail the buffalo herd watering down at the lake.

At the moment I'm talking about, however, Cisco was in a mood for riding a barstool. There was still plenty of time to hunt buffalo before snow flies.

"How is Pablo?" asked a waiter who overheard Charlie talking about his horse.

"I haven't seen that buckskin for a couple weeks," replied Charlie.

"The last time I seen him, out at Beecher's prairie, he was down in the meadow and the crows were trying to lift him," said the waiter.

"For paleface, you pretty funny," Charlie quipped.

Charlie bought a round, while his sister told us of an era when Williams Lake was only three houses and her baby brother Cisco Charlie "wasn't as high as a duck's ass." She recalled the time when she was alone at the cabin and heard a scratching at the window. She got out of bed and lit a lamp. A grizzly was standing at the cabin window. There was a rifle on the wall, but in her panic she picked up a double-bitted axe and started chopping. She damn near killed Charlie, who had been holding up the head of a grizzly he had shot a couple of days earlier. Charlie had to spend the next half-hour plugging up that cabin window in minus-thirty degree weather. He damn near froze but never got any sympathy from his big sister.

"Remember when Klingor got murdered?" asked Charlie.

"Who's Klingor?" said his sister.

"He was the one that killed old Burton's pigs."

Charlie started reminiscing about how hard he used to work, but his sister interjected.

"You was the laziest bastard from here to Vancouver."

"I had eighteen kids," shot back Charlie, "so I musta done some work."

"Yeah, and that's the only goddam work you ever done, too," his sister replied. It seemed that Charlie's sister had a typical teenaged daughter. "I wait on that girl hand and foot," said Charlie's sister, "and what do I get? Shit and bugger-all."

Attention was drawn to a magnificent pair of horns hanging over the bar. "I had a bull with horns like that," said Charlie, "we could hardly load him in the truck."

His sister piped up again, "Billy Joe and Frank Baker was fighting Saturday. Frank kept hitting him, but Billy wouldn't go down. The Mounties come by, and I took Billy home. He was bleedin' pretty bad. He soaked four towels, so I told him he better go to the hospital. He went, and they sewed him up."

"I used to own half the property in Williams Lake," said Charlie, "but it don't matter none. I came with nothin', and I ain't takin' nothin' with me."

I said to my wife that if we wanted to make 100 Mile House for supper we'd better get rolling. Along the way, we picked up an Indian cowboy and dropped him off in Lac La Hache. He was a lot quieter than Charlie. Matter of fact, he only said three words: "Nice car" and "Thanks." (No, make that four words. When I said, "Are you going to Lac La Hache?" he said, "Yep.")

Picking up that chap reminded me of another day when I stopped for an Indian kid (nowadays I call anybody under fifty a kid) who was hitching from Lac La Hache towards Williams Lake. "Where are you headed?" I asked. He gave a little self-conscious laugh and told me he was going to the Stampede at Williams Lake.

"Are you working around here?" I asked.

He gave another barely-audible giggle and said, "I was workin' for a rancher back of Lac La Hache, but I just left and didn't tell him I was goin'."

"How long did you work there?"

"Three months."

"Didn't you get paid?"

"No, I just left early this morning to go to the Stampede. They thought I was just goin' to Lac La Hache."

"Are you goin' back after the Stampede?"

This time he gave a real big laugh and said, "Nope."

At the time, I thought he must have a screw loose. He just lost three months wages, he takes off to go to the rodeo, and he still figures he pulled one off on the rancher. Now, I'm not all that certain this kid was nuts. After all, it's not every day one can see a Stampede. On the other hand, a guy can work on a ranch any old time. It's just a matter of priorities.

The Last Great White Hunter

The beginning of the end of my hunting career occurred in a slough in the middle of a hay field on my parents' farm in Aldergrove, BC. I had just shot the male mallard of a single pair of ducks who had claimed that patch of mosquito-infested green puddle for their own. I nailed him with an old single-shot .22 (the Ducks Unlimited, "get 'em in the air, give 'em a sporting chance" philosophy didn't apply then).

Now shooting things out of the air with six-shooters and rifles is great for Hollywood, but it never made a whole hell of a lot of sense to a hungry pioneer. They shot 'em on the ground or in the water. The problem was that I didn't fit either of those descriptions, not even the hungry part. And when that female mallard made about four low passes back over that pond as if she was trying to lift her mate, who was still struggling in the water, I started to do a little contemplating on this hunting business.

The simple truth was I didn't need to eat that damn duck. I rationalized the whole deal by saying my dad was crazy about wild duck. But forty years later, I can still see that dedicated female passing over the pond. Like I say, that was just the beginning of the end. The end of the end came several years later in the jack pine forest a dozen miles outside Lac La Hache.

I was carrying an old lever-action Winchester .30-.30 saddle gun, loaned to me by Teddy Hamilton, brother of Buster, the big game guide in that area. Teddy, another chap and I drove out to a spot where Teddy said he had good luck finding deer in years past. Teddy had a game leg, so he got out where the brush wasn't too thick and the hillside not too steep. Then he said us two should head in off the road at couple-hundred-yard intervals. That way, he said, if one person scared up a buck, it might head into the guns of one of the other two.

Boy, this was it. I was "big game hunting" for the first time. I headed into the bush between the other two hunters. Thinking back, it probably wasn't the safest spot. An old hunter like Teddy was unlikely to mistake me for a deer, but the other guy was new to hunting and I forgot to tell him that deer have four legs, short tails and a chair on their heads, leastwise the bucks do.

It was early in the morning and a light frost still covered the ground. Squirrels were throwing down pinecones all over the damn bush. I had walked in maybe a quarter mile when I heard this thumping on the ground. I learned later that when deer get exited they stamp their front feet, but at the time I didn't know what it was. I walked another few yards and there, not more than a hundred feet away, was a magnificent buck. I shot it just behind his shoulder and he went down behind a small rise.

I walked over the rise figuring he would be dead. Well, that buck was lying down all right but he was holding his head high. He was a beautiful animal, the kind you see in movies or life insurance ads. He was looking right at me and with every breath he took, steam and blood came out his side into the frosty air. I had shot him through the lungs.

Making the first shot was no problem. But now, ten feet away, with him looking right at me, it was a whole different ball game. Nevertheless, I shot him once more in the head and went to cut his throat. Then I discovered that I hadn't brought a knife.

Imagine! Hunting without a knife. Not to worry, I thought, there is a knife in the tackle box back in the car.

Now I faced two tasks: how to find my way to the road, and how to find my way back to the deer. I headed in the direction of the road, breaking off a small branch every few yards in order to find my way back. Twenty minutes later, I spied the gravel road through the trees and quickly found the car. The tackle box was in the trunk of my '49 Ford but my super-sharp fish-gutting knife was missing. I waited ten minutes figuring maybe Teddy or the other guy might show up, but no such luck. I'd have to make do myself.

Under the seat, I found a small hand axe of the type used for cutting kindling. Twenty minutes later, I got back to the deer and crudely cut his throat. Deer hide is damn tough, I soon found out. After rassling the carcass around so the head was downhill, I headed back to the car. It was starting to get warm so I hurried, figuring we should soon dress that deer.

When I got back to the car, both Teddy and the other guy were there having a smoke. They asked me if I saw anything, and what the shooting was about. I told them I had gotten a big buck and the three of us headed back, Teddy using his .30-.30 like a walking stick.

I must have somehow got screwed up in my directions that last trip; no damn way could I find the deer. Teddy was in his late sixties, and scrambling all over that bush was really bothering his bad leg. I felt bad for him and was madder than hell at myself for getting lost. I suppose the madder I got, the less chance I had of finding the deer. The sun was rising along with my blood pressure, and I was starting to panic for putting this poor old bugger through torture. We must have stomped around a good hour before we finally stumbled onto the buck.

The other guy and I rolled the carcass up on its back and Teddy slit the belly and gutted it. The head we left on as the antlers would be handy for towing. Then we set off. After dragging that buck a quarter-mile we were beat; I realized why some guys only hunt along the road.

We finally got to the car, loaded the deer into the trunk, and took it to the game-cutting and freezer plant at 100 Mile House. It dressed out at over two hundred and forty pounds.

Later, I gave Teddy back his .30-.30.

"I won't be borrowing this anymore," I said.

"Why not?" he asked.

"Well, when I come up over that rise, the deer was lyin' there just like a picture, lookin' at me as if to say, 'What in hell did you do that for?' And I'm thinkin', 'I don't have to do this to eat. Matter of fact, I don't even care much for deer meat'."

No Teddy, I'm afraid you are looking at the last of the Great White Hunters. That was the end of the end, period.

Taming the Similkameen

*L*iving in North Vancouver without a boat (as I had done for some time) can result in a person developing an inferiority complex. So I decided to buy something that could float. Little did I realize that in order to purchase even a modest craft, you have to mortgage your house, horse, dog, kids and the VCR.

After a long time (ten, maybe fifteen minutes), I decided a canoe would be the ticket. I chose a sturdy sixteen-foot fiberglass model, moulded in the style of the famous Frontiersman. It weighed only slightly less than the *Queen Mary*, but I figured the risk of the odd hernia or heart attack was worth it.

For our inaugural trip Midge and I took the canoe to Mosquito Creek, which runs into Burrard Inlet. The launching itself was smooth enough but once we got floating down the creek, two conclusions clearly manifested themselves: 1) canoes really don't like people, even though they look pretty on postcards, and 2) always take the rear-paddle position. That way you get to steer where you want. And if you do slack off and look at the scenery, the person in the front can't tell.

We had several other sea trials and they went without mishap, unless you count the time at Cates Park when Midge broke the cardinal rule of canoe-docking by putting one foot in the canoe and one foot on the float. The bow moved away, and down between the dock and the canoe, in slow motion, went Midge into fifteen feet of cold Pacific Ocean.

Midge soon bobbed to the surface, looking something like a harbour seal. Another fellow and I hauled her out easily; what wasn't so easy, however, was keeping a straight face. I know better than anybody, Hell hath no fury like a woman scorned, but this was too much.

On the way back home, Midge was strangely silent. We travelled through the scenic Burrard Reserve, past the tiny cemetery. Man, it was peaceful. Not a solitary word. I was thinkin', "If a guy has a wife that talks too much, he should take her on the odd canoe ride." Just thinkin' it, mind you.

After a hot shower and a hot rum, Midge sort of thawed out. I suggested, part in jest, that seeing as we were now seasoned veterans in the art of canoeing, we should leave the placid Pacific behind and try a little white water in the Okanagan. To my eternal surprise, she said yes. Either she has a helluva short memory, or she's as crazy as I am.

Now about halfway between the Okanagan towns of Princeton and Keremeos, right on the banks of the Similkameen River, friends of mine from North Vancouver had purchased acreage with tourist cabins and campsites. The Similkameen is a beautiful, crystal clear little river that borders the cattle ranches and campgrounds on the highway.

Our plan was to drop the canoe at my friend's place and drive the pickup to Keremeos, which was downstream about thirty miles. I'd leave the truck there and take the bus or hitchhike back to the campsite. That way our canoe trip would be all downstream.

We stopped off at the campsite and told my friend about our plans. "Sounds great," said Kenny. He informed us that we could find his brother and wife at the Keremeos Legion and catch a ride back with them. A good night's sleep, and we'd be on our way down the river.

Well, between a ride with a bunch of drunks in a rickety car, and several late-night interruptions, including a rainstorm and cars doing doughnuts in the gravel near our campsite, we didn't get much rest that night. But when we awoke, at about four-thirty, it looked as though the day was going to make up for it. It was a clear, crisp morning—perfect for a big trip. I fired up the Coleman stove and we had bacon and eggs, toast and coffee. I tried a couple of casts with a wet fly, no luck; but what a country, and what a spot!

We slid the canoe down the bank and loaded the lifejackets, boxes, paddles and fishing gear. Our first real white water lay ahead. Midge was silent and looked apprehensive, as if she was walking to the gallows. Because I'm the macho guy, I have to make most of the noise and play this little escapade down. Secretly though, I'm wondering if my will is in order. Would the kids have enough cash for our funerals?

Launching time at last. It was six-fifteen.

Midge picked up about an eight-foot pole a couple inches in diameter. For a few seconds I thought she was planning on collecting my life insurance. Then, without a word, she laid the pole in the canoe. "What's that for?" I asked.

"In case we have to pole our way along someplace."

"Good idea," I said, thinking I was humouring her.

I untied the bowline, flipped the canoe and steadied it till Midge got in. No chance to fall between the dock and the boat this time. The water was squeaky-clean, and the river was running pretty fast; soon we were coasting along at quite a clip. No paddling for these adventurers. It was just a case of keep the bow straight, enjoy the scenery and avoid the occasional rock. What a way to spend a holiday!

The first mile or two went smoothly. Then we hit a stretch of rapids and went like hell over some rocks that were very near the surface. We bumped a bit, but the canoe was fiberglass and it didn't do any damage. Hell, I thought, we're ready for Niagara Falls.

A half-mile further, we neared a spot where a highway

bridge crossed the river. It was a rough-looking section with lots of huge rocks and whirlpools. We got about one-third of the way in and hit a rock pretty hard. Then we hit another rock. And another, and another. Suddenly, the canoe jumped sideways and wedged solid between two massive boulders. We could hear the fiberglass cracking from the pressure of the water boiling against the side. The canoe started to roll lower and lower on the upstream side, and I knew as soon as the gunwale got below the water, it was gonna fill up and flip. If that happened, we were going to get bashed to hell on those rocks. I also knew that if we survived—which I was beginning to doubt—I planned to see a shrink and have my head examined.

While all this was happening, Midge remained silent. Of course, she was more religious than me and knew she would have a place to go to. She almost looked serene, or maybe petrified.

Desperate, I tried wedging us off with the paddle. Nothing. All the while, the canoe was still making cracking noises from the strain. Thank all the gods for fiberglass. Cars were stopping on the bridge ahead, taking advantage of a rare opportunity to watch two nuts commit suicide before their very eyes.

Time was running out. The canoe was gonna break any second. Just then, I saw the pole that Midge had thrown in. Levering the pole against that slippery rock, I started to slowly inch the canoe back into the mainstream. Now the problem was knowing that if I did pry us clear, we'd be going through the remaining rapids backwards, totally out of control.

Still, we couldn't stay till the canoe broke or rolled under. So I kept prying. Why didn't those damn people on the bridge go away? A dozen more pries, inch by inch, and suddenly the back end broke clear and down we went backwards, crashing into and over at least a dozen more boulders. Then, just as suddenly, we were free—the water turned dead flat and we paddled leisurely under the bridge. Nothing to it.

The sun was hot and our clothes were steaming. Was this

how Edmund Hillary felt? Midge looked smug and said, "You're lucky I brought that stick."

Believe it or not, for the next couple of miles the water was so shallow we had to drag the canoe along from shore with the bowline. But we had had enough fun for the day. We pulled the canoe up near the highway and walked to a small store. The storekeeper gave us a bus schedule, then said, "Where did you come from?" We said we had canoed down the river. "Alone?" We said yes. He was amazed. "But nobody canoes that river alone and nobody ever goes down this time of year."

Apparently Kenny has a strange sense of humour.

Anybody wanna buy a canoe?

IV.

Pots Pureed

What's in a Name?

Shakespeare said, "A rose by any other name would smell as sweet." Fair enough—let's change the name "rose" to "puke." Now, when you love a girl you send her a dozen long-stemmed pukes (if you're a cheap bastard, like me, you send her a single long-stemmed puke and tell her it's the thought that counts, and not the quantity). Imagine a puke-covered garden with the pukes climbing over the white trellis. How about putting a puke in your lapel and inviting all your friends to smell it? I don't know about you, but for me it just don't seem to fly.

A song came out in the sixties about a guy named Sue who planned to lay a beating on his father for hanging such a moniker on him. While the name Jim never gave me cause to try and ambush my old man (he was too big anyway), I should have taken both my parents aside and suggested they could have given me something more imaginative to carry through life.

Because my mother always had the King James version of the Bible within striking distance, I could understand her picking a biblical name for me. Although before she was born she had the good sense to pick for herself the name Ursula, which thereafter became Ushi.

My main beef was with my dad, who was born just west of Battleford, Saskatchewan, which is surrounded by three Indian reserves. His father and grandfather were both captured by the Indians and later charged with treason by the government for siding with the natives; my father spoke fluent Cree. With plenty of Indian friends, including Cree chief Adam Fineday, why didn't Dad ask the old chief to come up with a name for me?

The list of names below, which I lifted from an old Saskatchewan *Herald* newspaper, is of Indians around Battleford involved in the Riel rebellion. Maybe the old chief would have suggested some of these names: Dressy Man. Miserable Man. Lucky Man. Lean Man. Poundmaker. Sweet Grass. Wandering Spirit. Four Sky Thunder. Walking In The Sky. Yellow Mud Blanket. Strike Him On The Back. Breaking Through The Ice. Rattlesnake Dog.

Just imagine Mr. and Mrs. Yellow Mud Blanket signing in at a hotel. Never would anyone forget my name. So from now on, Dad, it's "Walking In The Sky." You can call me Jim, for short.

So what did I call *my* son? Not James, nosirree. I called him Roderick James. You see, my dad's first name was Roderick, so maybe paleface do speak with forked tongue. My daughter, Tobie, on the other hand, was lucky. If she had been born a boy, it would have been Rattlesnake Dog.

Ape-olution

One Sunday I went for a stroll through the Stanley Park Zoo. This is not your ordinary iron-cage-filled-with-psychotic-animals type of zoo. Nosirree, this is your high tech, free-form, natural habitat zoo where the animals, with the exception of those who have a habit of eating each other, mingle freely.

I checked out the monkeys, otters, bears, wolves and seals. They were all pretty laid back; it looked to me like they didn't work on Sunday either.

Eventually, I came to the place for the apes. They were in a real natural and authentic-looking jungle, right down to the concrete trees with fiberglass leaves. Well, I always like to see what our ancestors are up to, so I sat on a genuine reproduction wooden bench, placed my genuine reproduction German camera beside me, checked my genuine Japanese reproduction Swiss watch and unslung my Bausch and Lomb "Made in Hong Kong" binoculars. Just me and the raw elements in the deepest jungle of Stanley Park.

It was a tad chilly, and I could have used a fur coat like them apes wear. Still, being at the zoo was a whole hell of a lot better than sitting in church listening to a genuine reproduction of an authentic translation of the Bible.

Anyway, I saw this big ape was sitting eight, maybe ten feet up a concrete tree. Directly below him sat a smaller ape. As I watched, the big ape broke off a ten-pound branch (yes, ten pounds; he was from the old school) and dropped it smack on the head of the lower ape. Well, I thought, accidents will happen even in Apeland.

The bottom ape let out a whimper, rubbed his head a few times and went back to contemplating his belly button or the universe or maybe even banana heaven. Meanwhile, the ape on top climbed down and checked out his buddy. It was a real touching scene, yes sir, real touching. Then the big ape picks up that chunk of concrete, climbs back up the tree, gets directly over the other ape's head, and lets gravity do the rest. BAM! Right on the old noggin again.

Now the poor bugger down below has two lumps on his head and he's jumping around, more than a little pissed off. Down comes the big ape once more, picks up the concrete, and climbs back up the fake tree. By now they really have my attention. Surely the ape down below is gonna move. Unless he's been eating fermented bananas.

The next part astounded me. Just as the top guy let go, that bottom ape grabbed an empty feed bucket and placed it on his head. BAM! Another direct hit. But this time the branch bounced harmlessly off the bucket. Other than a little ringing in the ears, the lower guy suffered no ill effects.

The big ape climbed down, ignoring the little ape, and walked over to the fence near where I was sitting. Apparently the game was over.

I said to the big ape, "What do you call this game?"

"We call it 'Defence and Offence'."

"Do you ever change sides?"

"No, never."

"Why not?" I asked.

"Because I'm bigger than the other ape and I make the rules. And besides, I don't like getting those lumps on my head."

I said, "Maybe that little ape doesn't like getting those lumps on his head either."

The big ape thought for a minute. "Well," he said, "for one thing, that little ape ain't too bright, and in his tribe, life is cheap. He just don't look at things the way we do. Besides, the game is good."

"How is this game 'good'?" I asked.

"Well, it goes something like this: I drop a rock on this—I don't like to use the word 'ape'—on this bozo's head. He gets one, two, maybe three lumps on his head and has to go to the lump man to get his head fixed."

"The lump man?" I asked.

"Jeez, you homo saps sure as hell ain't all that quick," he says. "If you guys evolved from us, things must have gone backwards. I'll make this as simple as possible. I crack this bozo, he goes to the lump man. The lump man fixes his head. After the bozo's lumps are fixed, he has to pay the lump man thirty, maybe forty bananas. The lump man then takes the bananas home to his wife and all those snot-nosed little apes. Being a doctor you'd think he would know a little more about family planning, but that's another story. So the lump man gets paid, and that's good."

"What else?" I asked.

"Hell, that's just the beginning. The lump man has to have a place to fix lumps, and lots of apes get bananas to build these lump-fixing places. What's more, the lump man needs lump helpers, mostly she-apes, and they get bananas too; not many, but they get some. Occasionally, if I crack a bozo a good one, he lies real still and a couple other apes lay him on a board and carry him away. Even them jerks get bananas. The amount of good I do for society by beaning those dumb bastards on the head travels outward like ripples on a pond. Do you understand?" he asked.

"Hell, yes," I replied.

"Do you homo saps have a game like that?"

"Hell yes," I said again.

"What do you call it?" asked the ape.

"War."

This Old House—A Horror Story

Millions of TV viewers across this land watch a series about renovating, landscaping, cabinet-making and construction of all sorts on a series called "This Old House." Presumably the intent of the program is to give all and sundry the basic skills to transform a teetering shambles into a palace in three or four easy stages.

Now my wife and everyone else's wife residing on Planet Earth watch this master carpenter, Norm, work his magic with the wood and the power tools right there before their very eyes, all in the space of one half-hour. (And never ever, I repeat, never, does he make a single bloody mistake. I could gladly strangle the guy.)

"Why can't you do that, honey?" asks my wife, after watching Norm build a grand piano out of a bunch of packing crates. What the program fails to explain is that Norm has four million dollars worth of power tools. Everything is sharp, he can measure things correctly, and he can saw straight. He's a good carpenter, sure, but he's got a lot of high tech help.

"I can't be good at everything," I remark to my wife, while Norm French-polishes a timber he found under a railway bridge.

"How about settling for one thing?" remarks my smart-ass wife.

One day my wife decided she wanted a 6x6-inch picture framed with old barn wood. We were going through an "old barn wood" stage at the time, so I found some old 1x8-inch cedar board on an ancient broken-down fence. Strictly speaking, it wasn't barn wood, but I wasn't about to tell anyone if she didn't.

I took one of these old cedar boards that were ten feet long and ripped it on the table saw into one-inch strips. Now I had sixty linear feet of one-inch potential picture frame moulding. All I needed was enough to go around a six-inch-square picture. About three linear feet should have been ample; after all, four times six is only twenty-four. So on a three-foot length, I should have had enough material left over to start a fire in the stove.

The only problem was that the corners on that picture frame had to be cut at forty-five degree angles, and I've never had much luck with forty-five degree angles. My bright friends tell me that four equal lengths cut at forty-five degrees will make a square. That's easy for them to say, with all their bloody book-learnin' and theories. Reality is much more tricky.

About forty linear feet and three hours later, the frame was ready. What's more, some of those angles actually touched in a couple of places. My wife said, "It's not as neat a job as Norm does on TV."

I said, "Yeah, but I bet Norm can't play the trumpet. And besides, look at all the kindling I got to light the fire!"

Have You Got a Pocketknife?

"Have you got a pocketknife?" my dad asked me one day. Not, "Have you got a jackknife?", or just, "Have you got a knife?" but, "Have you got a pocketknife?" In my dad's time it was a "pocketknife," period.

As luck would have it, I was carrying my "pocketknife." It was an old knife I had found while nosing through some stuff in the local dump twenty years before. In my time, garbage dumps were not sacrosanct and out of bounds. Consequently, every time I went to the dump I would come back with more than I took. It's a nasty habit I still haven't shaken.

Anyway, this was a well-used old knife, curved to fit comfortably in the hand, with a solid wood, riveted handle. From the look of it, it probably had belonged to an old farmer. The larger of the two blades was so thin it must have cut the twine on ten thousand bundles of cow feed. "Have I got a pocketknife?" Damn right.

The blade must have been sharpened a thousand times, completely eliminating the name of the manufacturer. Steel like that had to have come from Germany or Sweden, maybe even

Sheffield. I figured I had put a pretty fair edge on her a couple days previous, so I fished the knife out of my pocket and handed it to my dad. He studied it, then turned it over slowly two or three times in his gnarled old hands. How many hay bales had he opened on the dairy farm back home with just such a knife?

Back and forth along its length he ran a blackened thumb, long since turned to leather by sixty years of tamping down burning McDonald's Brier tobacco in his pipe. As a kid I was continuously fascinated by those farmers tamping down glowing red-hot tobacco with a thumb. I even tried it myself, once.

Without a word, and easy as pie, he snapped opened the large blade, which despite the age and wear was still strongly sprung. I had thought briefly of opening it for him, but hell, a man has to be left with some dignity.

He ran his thumb slowly along what I thought was a damn fine edge. I knew right along what he was thinkin'. He was thinkin', "So you run into a saber-tooth or a grizzly with that thing and you ain't even goin' to give him a vaccination." He kept running his thumb along that edge, then said, "You should have a stone. You should always carry a small stone."

My dad's not around anymore to ask if I carry a "pocket-knife," but he wouldn't have to worry. I pack one all the time. It's the same knife and it's damn sharp, just in case anyone asks. Or if I run into a grizzly. I also bought a small stone. I don't carry it in my pocket, but I always keep it handy.

One day I'm going to ask my son, "Do you have a pocket-knife?"

Sleep Walkin'

"To sleep perchance to dream," said the Bard. Far be it from me to correct that learned gentleman, especially at this late date. But if I were him, I would have changed it to something like, "To sleep or not to sleep, that is the question."

Most of my friends (all two of them) say they are sick of the bloody questions, they just want an answer. How to sleep? I say don't come to me. I can't get to sleep either.

I've used every trick and devious device ever invented to help people sleep. I've read every book, I've taken all the courses, done all my homework. Still, nothing works.

Now take my dog. He can be going three hundred miles an hour chasing cats, cars, kids or cows, and a half-second later he is flat on the ground making little strange yelping noises, twitching and chasing some damn rabbit deep, deep in dreamland. Oh, for a dog's life.

There is one guaranteed way to get me to sleep—driving. I get the car a half-mile down the freeway and—you guessed it—I'm fighting the urge to zonk off. So I drive less than a mile, pull off the road, and shut off the car. Now I'm wide awake.

My wife says, "What did you stop for?"

I say, "The modulator valve in the transmission is sticking," or, "A back wheel came off a while ago and I'm waiting for it to catch up."

"Do you want me to drive?" she asks. "Well, okay," I say, and slide over to the passenger side.

We start off again. I tilt the seat back. Now I'm really wide awake, and terrified too.

You figure it out.

Cashing It In

I know everybody has their bad days, but sometimes a little nagging something tells me the devil may be working overtime in my corner, especially in the supermarket, where he's always just ahead of me at the cash register.

Can anyone out there identify with this? I have one article to go through and there's no express lane—nothing as sophisticated as that—however there are six cash registers, but five have lineups just short of Newfoundland and I live in Vancouver. The sixth cash register has two people, count them, two people to go through—and each has only one article. Well, I'm no fool, I take the sixth till. Okay, so I'm in lane six, and the first person lays that single article down. The clerk runs it over the scanner and no beep, runs it over again and still no beep, looks for the price, there is none, asks the customer and the customer says "All I know is it's fifty percent off." The clerk picks up her mike and calls for a price check.

Meanwhile, I'm watching that Newfoundland line, it's down around Toronto, and I'm thinking, surely I didn't pick the wrong line. The call comes back on the mike—that article is not on sale anymore—and that's why the scanner doesn't pick it up. The woman protests, saying, "I have the flyer right here."

The next line is now down to Winnipeg and I'm still thinking of moving over but hell, I got time invested in this line. Finally the first customer gets through, now I'm sailing. I still picked the right line. One down, one to go. Her single article scans okay, the other lines are around Hope, BC, and it's all downhill from Hope.

The lady pulls out a cheque! A cheque—it can't be, it's only one article. She makes out the price, forgets to write in the amount and doesn't know the date, the other lines are down to about North Burnaby. The clerk asks for two pieces of identification. That's it, I jump the line, no more problems, I'm the last guy in the store. The clerk runs out of tape, everyone else is gone. I'm thinking, they shoot horses, don't they?—maybe there's a painless sort of suicide.

Well, I've run that play out a thousand times, but one day I thought of a way I could get some advantage out of my supermarket jinx.

I'm in the store and I see this jerk I used to work with. Now is my chance to get this turkey. I feign friendliness, ask about the family and all that crap, and get in line just ahead of him. I have twenty-seven articles and he has three, now he's gonna find out what I been putting up with all my life.

Bam, I'm right through. Every item scans perfectly, I can't believe it. I hand the clerk a cheque and say "Don't you want some ID?"

"No, I've seen you in here a hundred times."

Since I had three bags of groceries to pack, the chap I had planned to screw up was out the door before I was, so I wished him a merry Christmas. If I'm gonna have a jinx, I wish it was a jinx I could rely on.

Lying and Dying

He passed away. She expired. They went to their reward. He's gone. I put my dog to sleep. Passed over. Out of their misery. Gone to their maker. Gone to heaven. Nobody dies anymore, nobody dies.

It's like the joke about the grandson who keeps saying to his grandfather, "Make a noise like a frog, Grandpa, make a noise like a frog." Finally the grandfather asks the child, "Why?" and the child says, "Mommy says when you croak, we get to buy that new car."

People croak, but nobody dies.

I've spent years (okay, hours) contemplating this phenomenon. As far as I can figure, all my good friends who have passed away are now dead. Not only have they died, each one has taken a piece of me. Some left gaping holes, some left small abrasions, but each and every one has taken a piece of me.

Each time we bury someone, we learn, or relearn, that life is fragile and short. We also learn we're all on the same train. Television, one of the greatest and most misused inventions of the century, graphically reminds us of death and dying. Air disasters, highway carnage, shipwrecks, fire, earthquakes, famine and war; hundreds of scenes of slow or sudden death flash across our screens daily.

If we lie about our age, we lie about our birth, so I reckon a little lyin' about dyin' is normal. I think most of us don't want to lose too many pieces.

There's an old Western song by Ernest Tubb called "Waltz Across Texas." We waltz across life as if it's a rehearsal. We seem to think that if we don't get it right the first time we'll get to do it again. I hate to throw cold water on that scenario, but if life is the rehearsal, the play is generally cancelled.

I can handle it when an old friend with lots of mileage dies. It's the young, the sick and victims of accidents that are harder to take. One of the hardest deaths for me to accept was one I saw years ago in a news clip from Vietnam, where a totally obscene, totally unnecessary war was being rained on a poverty-stricken peasant population.

A peasant was burying a son who had been killed in a bombing raid. The soldiers standing around had given the man an army blanket in which to bury the child. The child was two, maybe two and a half years old, and the father had dug a shallow grave and placed the blanket down with that baby on it. The worst part was that the man seemed unable to decide at which position or angle to cross the child's hands on his chest. He must have changed the position four or five times before he covered that body. I knew he was stalling for time.

That baby didn't pass away, that baby didn't expire. That baby was murdered.

It was totally obscene and it left a huge hole.

The Wood Stove

With my electric stove and microwave oven, waxing romantic about wood stoves is simple. Still, the one long suit of the wood stove is time. They have a friendly, don't-rush-me-buster attitude not found in modern appliances. A wood stove has time.

Can anyone nowadays relate to a stove that keeps a meal warm two or three hours, and the meal is still as good as new? Can anyone relate to a stove that makes real toast, dries your socks and heats your house, all in one operation?

A meal on a wood stove is not just an accomplishment, it's a philosophy.

Recycling

I'm wearing a pair of crocheted slippers my mother made before she died, some twenty-two years ago. I have modified them by adding a couple of moosehide soles cut from a discarded jacket I found, and by darning them several times with the wrong-coloured wool. Nevertheless, the slippers are for the most part as good as the day my mother made them—from wool unravelled from a discarded sweater. My mother was Swiss, and to the Swiss, waste is a sin.

Folks run around today preaching the great new philosophy of recycling as though they invented the bloody concept. Hell, they should have spent a little time with my Swiss mother, or any of those early pioneer immigrants. They would have learned the practice, not just the theory, of making things last.

In the old days, on the rare occasion when anything was bought new, it was usually for the eldest kid in those large families. This process was damn disconcerting to the younger kids, to say the very least. But it made perfect sense in an era when kids came quicker than cash.

Here's how the system worked: the oldest and largest kid would get a new shirt. As soon as he grew out of it, it was handed down—and patched if need be—to the next in line. This went on until the shirt resembled one of them patchwork quilts. And that's exactly where anything salvageable wound up, after the buttons were removed. Any scraps left over were used as wiping rags for working on machinery. When the rags were so dirty as to be of no further use, they were used to light the fire. The ashes from the fire were used in the garden, or to make soap, or to keep the flies down in the outhouse. That was recycling in a time when nobody knew how to spell "recycling," much less knew what it meant.

I know the younger generation invented sex, but recycling, UH-UH.

Talkin' to Myself

As a kid, I regarded anyone who talked to themselves as a bit eccentric at best, or, at worst, as a criminally insane person who had possibly just escaped from the Provincial Mental Hospital a few miles away.

Years later I analyzed this behavior. I wondered if there are any grey areas. For instance, is it okay to sing by yourself? If so, is it okay to sing loudly by yourself? Or must you keep it to pianissimo? (If you can't carry a tune in a bucket, it's likely beneficial if you do sing quietly.) Such conundrums should never be taken lightly. A man needs to know when his bubble gets a little off-plumb.

The other day, I was working alone, building a fence, when I hit my thumb with the hammer. Without realizing I was by myself, I said, "Son of a bitch." Well, I marched right down to my shrink's office and confessed. "Son," he said, "as long as this is an isolated incident there may still be some hope. But if it ever happens again, phone for the ambulance immediately."

I thanked him profusely and gave him a hundred dollars. As I closed the door, I heard him exclaim loudly to himself, "Man, have I got myself some sweet racket."

That did it. I ran home and called a carpenter to come and fix the fence.

I hope to hell he doesn't hit his thumb with the hammer.

Kin Ya Card A Gitar, Bye?

Rufus Guinchard of Daniels Bay, Newfoundland, was one of Canada's best-loved and longest-surviving old-time fiddlers. In 1986, he received the Order of Canada, and I believe 99.9% of Canadians were happy to see that venerable chap given recognition for his many, many years of good old, down-East, foot-stompin' fiddling.

My wife and I once attending a play (I believe the show was called *Paper Wheat*, but don't quote me) at the Vancouver East Cultural Centre. Anyway, Rufus Guinchard and three other musicians were there, providing old-time music.

The play was great, but the highlight of the show for me was the good old-time music and the fiddling of Rufus Guinchard. It brought back lots of memories of the dances we had back in Saskatchewan in the old Eight Mile Lake one-room schoolhouse, a few miles west of Battleford.

After the play was over, we were having a drink in the little lounge adjoining the stage when Rufus walked in and sat at the next table. I remarked to him how I enjoyed his music.

"Kin ya card a gitar, bye?" he said, which I took to mean, "Can you chord a guitar, boy?"

"Sure," I said.

"Go on back dere," he continued, "an git one o dem fellers to give you his gitar."

Now, out here in the staid old conservative west, we would never dream of asking a touring musician to borrow his instrument. The response would be to call the bouncer. Well, these Newfie musicians were not from the conservative west, as I soon found out when I timidly asked this chap to borrow his guitar.

"Hell yes, bye, an dere's anoder one too if ya needs it," he said, as he handed me his guitar.

Rufus was well into his eighties at that time, but we played for a good hour and a half. His energy was phenomenal. It was a real privilege to play with a gentleman who really lived for music—a man with real talent and a complete lack of ego.

Rufus lived to the ripe old age of ninety-one plus a day. He was still playing the fiddle, and I'll bet dollars to doughnuts the first question he asked Saint Peter was "Kin ya card a gitar, bye?"

I Want to Look at the Trees

I tiptoed around the foot of the bed, as quiet as a mouse on pile carpet. His eyes were almost completely closed. I was sure he was asleep. Then he said, "Are you having trouble with the car again? I thought you had left."

"I thought you were asleep, did I waken you?" I said. "I can't find my keys."

"No, I wasn't sleeping," he replied. "I was looking at the trees. I like to watch the trees."

Those bloody trees. How could a man be so crazy about trees after spending most of his life chopping them down and digging stumps?

"I thought you didn't like trees," I said. "You been telling me for years if you had any dang brains you woulda never taken up on this bloody stump farm to begin with, but stayed on the prairies like all your other smart relatives did."

He was quiet. I thought of the many times I had watched him work in the alder swamp with an axe you could shave with. "You always have to clean the area around the tree before you cut it down, in case some of those smaller branches catch the axe, and you could get hurt," he would say. "You kids go and sit over there, so this tree don't fall on you."

We would sit a few yards back as he swung that axe in full, smooth arcs, the head thunking into the alder. A second later, the echo came back from the far side of the ravine. With every second stroke of the axe, a chip would come out as thick as your hand, and when that tree went crashing down, we would run over to see a stump that was cut off clean, as though by some giant knife. It was bloody magic.

His gnarled hands now curled like land crabs on top of the patchwork quilt. They would cut no more alders. I wondered what happened to that old-razor sharp axe and what kind of edge was on it now. "Will you be all right?" I asked. "I won't be more than a couple hours. I put your cereal on the table, and there's fresh coffee on the stove."

"I'll be fine," he said. "Wasn't that a corker of a wind last night? The trees were bending right over."

I gathered up the car keys and left without answering. On the drive to town I wondered how long we could keep him. I wondered how much longer he would last. Damn this bloody ageing business anyway. I always knew kids were a problem, but parents too? Maybe it's just people that are the goddam problem, period.

In the old days in the north, when an Eskimo got real old, he or she would just walk out onto the ice and lie down and die. I used to think that was a terrible thing. Then I discovered what we do with our old people in North America. Now I'm not so sure.

When animals get old, other animals eat them. But frankly, I don't think the animals would have us, even if we did promise to upgrade our behavior. Besides, I was talking to a cannibal friend of mine and he told me old people are tougher than hell, no matter how long you marinate them.

Why in hell can't I face reality? He's old. He has to go. Why in hell do I feel guilty? I never gave him that much trouble and I ain't even Catholic anymore.

The following week we placed him in one of those warehouses for people we call old-age homes. You know, the ones where people shuffle along on walkers or sit in wheelchairs, staring at the floors or walls, waiting. They wait for kids who never show up; they wait for meals; they wait for bed time; they wait and yearn for the time when the waiting is past.

I fed him water through a straw in the last days, and he would tell me of his time with the Indians, of Riel, and of the prairies and his half-breed grandfather Charlie Bremner, who had a tenacious desire for justice and fair play.

The last time I went to see him I had to inform the nurse on duty that he had died. He died alone, in a room without windows, and he couldn't see the trees.

I hope he was dreaming of cutting alders in the swamp.

The Word

The Bible says, "In the beginning there was the word." The word is all we have, all we have is the word.

This word game gets confusing. Words change as a result of slang or because their meaning has been deliberately manipulated. Sometimes words are candy-coated to ease down the throat of poor old gullible John Q. Public. A good example is, "gone to their reward" instead of "died"; the Indians said someone had gone to the "happy hunting ground."

These changes don't take long. Even in my time, they used to sell "second-hand cars." Then some fella said, "We better dress that up a little; from now on they will be known as 'Used Cars'." Today, nobody in their right mind would buy, drive or even sell a used car, let alone a secondhand one. Nowadays, you buy only "Pre-Owned" automobiles. That's the only kind they sell, because they run better and they have class. Mind you, they do cost a little more. "Yes, Madam, you may now view our pristine selection of 'Pre-Owned Automobiles.' By appointment only, of course."

For straight flimflam—I almost said bullshit—it's hard to beat the real estate people. The peculiar language of their business is difficult to translate, but I'll give it a shot. "Rustic Location," means access by helicopter only. "Quaint," built by hippies out of driftwood and canvas in 1962. A "steal" means the seller is a bandit. "Handyman's Special," fit for pack rats only. "Needs a little TLC," needs a roof, foundation, walls, wiring, plumbing, windows, wallboard, insulation, and it's beside the tracks. "Can't last" means condemned by the health inspector. "Starter home"—the only way to fix this one is with a little starter fluid.

I remember the days when "bad" meant "not good"; nowadays, when you see a musician that's really cookin', people say "Man, he's real bad." Now that means he's real good. Bad, as in poor quality, is now "sub-optimal." "Cabin fever" is now "Seasonal Affective Disorder." The word "now" has been shortened to "at this particular point in time." Short people are no longer short, they are "vertically challenged." There used to be poor countries, now there are only "developing countries"; poor people are now simply "economically deprived." People don't get fired anymore, but some do get "dehired."

We don't say "old people"; we say "seniors." We don't say "birth defect"; we say a person has a "congenital disability." We don't say "cripple"; we say "a person with a mobility impairment." (I suppose we could say people who are dead have "mobility impairment.") We don't say "mentally retarded," we say "person with an intellectual disability." We don't have normal people any more, just "persons who are not disabled."

"Lazy" people have vanished too; now there are just some people who "suffer disincentive ambitions." In my time, when a guy didn't want to work, we called him a hobo, a bum or a lazy bastard, depending on our religion. Now when somebody doesn't want to work, they are "undermotivated." Is that better?

If my mom were around, she would say, "That's okay, son, I understand you're just a little 'undermotivated,' but tonight when we are having supper, you're going to be 'undernourished' besides."

I was on a boat the other day and the damn thing started sinking. I hollered for a lifejacket. This turkey hands me a "flotation device." I tell you, it's enough to make a man suffer "neurotic transmogrification." Hell, I can remember the time when I thought Shakespeare was a great wordsmith, but just think what he could have accomplished with our new terminology (provided, of course, he wasn't suffering from "disincentive ambitions").

The American army has always been a great one for this word game. They don't drop napalm or high-explosive bombs on people; they send down a little "ordinance." Nobody gets blown to hell anymore; they become "collateral damage." The term "shell shock" has been shortened to a "combat-related stress event."

If you were to make a list of the most prostituted words in the world, you'd have to include "love" of course, and "freedom" and "sale." But the one word that has really been getting to me lately is "obscenity." Just mention the word to most folk and they clasp their hands over their kids' eyes and ears, fearing something sexually explicit. Man the pulpits!

Obscenity hasn't got anything to do with sex. Obscenity is bloated bellies. Obscenity is flies walking over the eyes of not-yet dead kids who lack the strength to close their eyelids. Obscenity is Canada bulldozing apples and vegetables in landfills to keep prices up; it's Canada spending thirty-eight million dollars each for 135 outdated American fighter planes, while at the same time the country closes down hospital beds for lack of funds; it's a woman pregnant for the tenth time while some chubby cleric councils her on the evils of birth control.

Obscenity is supplying friendly dictators with arms so they can forever keep the peasants on their knees in poverty and misery. Obscenity is infant mortality in the millions from bad water in 1990, while we have the technology to live and travel in outer space; it is religious denominations of all stripes with their heads in the sand while the AIDS epidemic rages; it is the mind-numbing pabulum, crap and violence that's on television; it's people watching the stuff. Obscenity is billions spent on arms each year throughout the globe. Obscenity is TV evangelists with air-conditioned dog kennels taking money from hard-up old people.

Yes, Martha, we have enough obscenity around to last a thousand years. And it probably will, as long as we focus our energy on sexual frivolity, nudity and all that heavy stuff. I tell you, this word business is just too much, and that's not Bad and it's not Good either, if you get my meaning.

Does anyone know what the hell I'm talkin' about? Me neither.

V.

Some Folks I've Known

My Buddy Al Brown

Did you ever meet someone and immediately check the high numbers on your life's odometer and say, "damn, damn, damn. I wish I'd run into this character before my warranty expired?" Well I have, and that someone is Al Brown.

"Once I built a railroad," goes the beginning of the song. Well, the Al I know never built a railroad, but he has built a lot of boats. The last was the *Nicki Boat*, so named because it was for Nicaragua—that dirt poor Central American country trying to survive massive assaults on the peasant population by hired killers sponsored and armed by the USA.

The *Nicki Boat* project was born after Al and some friends sailed to Nicaragua. They landed at a remote fishing village called San Juan Del Sur and found conditions far worse than they had imagined. The people's boats were completely unseaworthy, their nets were shredded or nonexistent, and they had no method of holding fish in the heat for any length of time. The whole fishing industry was a shambles.

Having been a BC fisherman most of his life, Al could easily empathize with the poverty-stricken fishermen down there. Now lots of people have empathy with the poor and downtrodden, but empathy alone won't put beans in the pot. So Al says, "What we do is go back home and build them a boat, a good boat, a boat rigged for at least a half-dozen fishing operations." From time to time, Mr. Brown has been known to bullshit a little regarding his prowess at certain skills. But when it comes to boats and fishing, he is one of the best. That part ain't no BS.

So Al gets back to Vancouver and announces his plan. "But a boat like that would cost a minimum quarter-million," said the people he talked to. "How are those poor people ever going to afford something like that?"

"No problem," says my old buddy, "we'll get a few donations. I'll talk to my Indian friends who own and operate the marina in North Vancouver and arrange for space. Then I'll build a shed, build and rig the boat. When it's finished we'll send it down and give it to those fishermen. That settles the money question." When people asked about Al's time and labour, he said that was free too.

"Brown, you gotta be crazy."

"Yep," said Al, and his wife Norah agreed.

Three and a half years and thousands of man-hours later, the boat sits fully-rigged for trolling, gillnetting and dragging. It has enough donated nets to outfit half a dozen boats.

For the past year, between coffee breaks and tales of great fishing and seafaring exploits, I have been helping Al on the *Nicki Boat*. First off, whoever gets there in the morning has to light a fire in the big iron stove Al built in the front of the boatshed. While that old heater is getting up to speed, we go over to the Highboats Cafe, originally owned by our fishin' buddy Dave Lloyd, and now run by a couple of good-natured ladies who have heard way more fish stories than they probably ever cared to. Often Al and I join forces there with our good friend Barrie Farrel, whose concern for humanity is surpassed only by his skill in boat building.

Now, attempting to solve all the world's problems is no easy task, so we end up drinking at least three or four coffees every time we try. Before we get back to the shed, nine times out of ten one of them hundreds of other boat owners down there drags my partner away for advice on some problem or other. Whether the problem is mechanical, electrical, rigging, deck or hull, fiberglass, steel or wood, Al takes it all in stride and generally fixes the damn thing himself. Then it's time for another coffee and more politics, with just a sprinkling of bullshit thrown in for seasoning.

"If you charged consultation fees you would have more money than Melvin Belli," I keep telling him. But Al's never had much of a fascination with monetary matters. He still fishes a little each year, but that's just to keep the wolf from the door and to fulfill the requirements of his commercial licence.

Al reminds me of the guy who said, "I made a small fortune in the fishing industry, but of course I started with a large fortune." He has survived some pretty close calls, like the time when his boat blew up from a gasoline explosion just off West Vancouver near the Point Atkinson Lighthouse. He came to in the water with pieces of his boat still falling around him. When I suggested that he might be better off with a job that doesn't involve bobbing through hurricanes in a leaky old tub, he said, "No problem, only the good die young." (He could be right. I'm over twenty myself.)

Minor things like getting blown up, or sunk out there somewhere this side of Japan, don't concern Al. He has more serious matters to worry about, such as winning horse races. And with some of those refugees from the fox-food plants that Al claims out at the track from time to time, that's no mean feat.

"Why in hell don't you just stick with boats, where you know losin' money is a sure thing," I ask, "rather than fool with those damn horses, where you have the illusion of winnin' a race and makin' money sometimes?"

"Maybe one time those other seven horses in the race will get sick, or lightning might strike. Who knows?" says Al. Faced with such overwhelming logic, I usually give up and we go and have another coffee.

One morning Al arrived at work looking like he had just

survived a massive bombing raid. His knees and elbows were all skinned, he had a bruise on his head and he could hardly walk. It seems at dinner the previous evening his two daughters, who are both in their early twenties, were talking about jogging and sprinting and stuff like that. Al made a slight technical error by saying he didn't think they were as smart as they thought they were, and that he could outrun the both of them, even on one of his bad days. As it turned out, this wasn't one of his bad days.

After dinner they set up the race. It was to be one long block in front of the house. Now Al figured he would let his daughters have an early lead, then just at the last few yards he would blow by them, thereby proving that the ageing process is reserved strictly for all them other old buggers.

So the race began. He told me later, "Those turkeys could really run, but I figured I could still take them in the final yards." His strategy went afoul when he caught the toe of a sneaker in one of those tar strips between the slabs of the sidewalk. Down he went onto the concrete, where he lay all bruised and bleeding. His daughters thought he was dead, but his wife said he was just crazy. (Personally, I tend to agree with the latter.)

Al gets quite nostalgic at times and claims that the last good car was the Model A Ford. He also claims that all university and book learnin' does is teach people "the square root of a turkey's ass." To tell the truth, that's something I still can't figure out myself. I know something about turkeys, but square roots leave me cross-eyed. Maybe I should have gone to one of them universities myself.

Now Al smokes way more than is good for his health, my health or anyone else's health who is within fifty yards of his puffing. But when his friends complain about his habit he simply says Winston Churchill promised him that if he won the Second World War single-handed, he could smoke from then on as much as he damn-well pleased. He did, and so he smokes.

During the war Al was a stokerman on a Canadian corvette doing convoy duty in the North Atlantic. It was their job to get the German subs before the subs blew hell out of the freighters and tankers that were carrying supplies to the Allies. Sonar, or "asdic," was still an imperfect technology in those days, and consequently depth charges killed one hell of a lot more fish than submarines. But they had to work with what they had.

One day the captain of Al's corvette called the crew on deck and told them the brass suspected the Germans had some new kind of cork or tar lining their subs, making them almost impossible to detect. They were to capture the next sub they crippled and keep it afloat to study.

"Here's the game plan," said the captain. "After we locate and force a sub to the surface, we will need a boarding party, to be made up as follows: six seamen to row the boat and one stokerman to board the sub." The captain went on to explain that the stokerman would carry a Sten gun, four hand grenades, and a six-foot length of chain. The seamen would row over to the sub, and the stokerman would jump on board. When the hatch opened, he'd throw the chain part way down the hatch to prevent the sub from diving. Then the stokerman would threaten to throw down the grenades if the sub crew didn't come up peacefully.

"Now," said the captain, "we need a stokerman to volunteer." Al thought the plan was crazy, and apparently so did all the other stokermen because the silence was deafening. After thirty seconds, the captain started telling the crew they're a bunch of chicken-shit, pantywaist sissies and he wondered where the John Waynes were. That didn't do any good either. Not a volunteer.

"Okay you lily-livered bunch of bastards," snapped the captain. "I will choose a volunteer." He lined up the stokermen.

"Any A's?" Nothing.

"Let's try the B's . . . Brown, Al. Step forward! You have just volunteered for the boarding party!"

The next few weeks Al spent nearly every waking hour invoking strange curses, such as, "may the fleas of a thousand camels infest his arm pits," and "may his life be filled with lawyers," on his boss. He was hoping—no, praying—that the war would end, or that the captain would be called home by the big admiral in the sky, or that all them subs would run out of gas and go home. He was especially hoping they wouldn't wound a sub.

Two months pass, and still no solid contact with the enemy. Then early one morning the alarm sounds. The asdic has picked up a sub. There's panic, and numerous depth charges are launched over the aft end of the corvette. Al prays they either miss the sub altogether, or if they do hit it, that it sinks straight down to Davy Jones's locker. That way he wouldn't have to indulge his crazy captain.

All is quiet for a few minutes. Then, what do you know, not five hundred yards away the familiar sight of a conning tower starts to appear above the surface. "Holy Christ," thinks Al, "this is it."

"Boarding party stand by," hollers the captain.

Al's thinking, "Why in hell didn't I have a name farther up the alphabet, something like Weston or Xavier?" It's bad enough when you take a girl to a motel and the guy asks your name, and you say "Brown," and the guy looks at you and thinks, "You sure ain't very original. I get two hundred guys here named Brown or Smith every month." Hell, if his name was even Smith, he wouldn't have had to "volunteer" for this kamikaze mission.

So the boarding party lines up at the rail, and the boat is lowered over the side. Al's knees are knockin' worse than the bottom end of that rickety Model A Ford he left back home. They are just about to get into the boat, when the sub starts to sink—straight down.

Now, my friend had lots of mixed emotions. He didn't want to board that sub, but he also sure the hell didn't like to see the whole sub crew die in a fashion you wouldn't wish on a dog.

Al would be the first to agree that war is hell. He'd also second the motion that boarding parties wouldn't be all that much fun either.

Gary the Fiddle Man

My wife Gerry and I were returning from Langley Prairie to our home in North Vancouver one Saturday afternoon, and as we were crossing the Second Narrows Bridge, I suggested we drop in at the Lynnwood pub for "one" beer before dinner. We had a drink and were just about to leave when a dark-haired young guy walked onto the stage and began tuning his violin, which was sitting there from a previous set. He finished tuning and made one tiny pass down the strings. "We can't leave now," I said.

"Why not?" said Gerry.

"Cause that guy can really play."

"How do you know?" she asked. "He hasn't played anything yet."

"Yes he has."

Back in Saskatchewan, I used to play the guitar with several half-breed fiddlers at school dances and weddings and such. They were good, but I knew this guy was fantastic. So we stayed.

It turned out his name was Gary Comeau and he was playing with one hell of a guitar player named Nilan Ritter. The two of 'em were really smokin'. After the set I went up to the stage and told them how much I enjoyed their music and asked if I could buy them a beer. They agreed and sat down at our table, where we introduced ourselves and began talking about where they normally played, what kind of music they preferred and the music business in general.

"Do you play anything?" asked Gary.

"I play the guitar a little," I said. "But after hearing Nilan, I'm gonna go home and burn it."

"Can you sing?"

Now there's nothing like making a good first impression for a lasting friendship, so I said, "I can sing the ass off you two guys." My wife looked horrified. But Gary never even blinked.

"Okay," he said. "You're comin' up next set. You gotta have two songs."

"I only know one."

"You gotta know two."

"Well I know one song and an old spiritual, called 'Sinner Man'."

"Good enough."

Gary and Nilan returned to the stage and Gerry turned to me. "Have you ever sung on the stage before?" she said.

"Yep, one time in grade three at a Christmas concert."

"That's it?"

"Yep, that's it."

"Aren't you scared?"

"Hell no," I said, lyin' real bad. It's one thing to do crazy things on the spur of the moment, but it's a whole different story when you really stick your neck out and somebody calls your bluff, and there you are, hoist on your own petard. So I'm acting real cool, pretending to enjoy my beer, but secretly I'm dyin'. I hope that Gary is having a little fun,and really doesn't plan to ask me up after all.

Next thing he announces over the mike, "I want you to put your hands together for a special guest who is gonna come up and sing a couple of songs."

That walk up there was the longest walk of my life. Me and

my big mouth got me into this jackpot. Special guest, indeed. The worst part was I had known several of the people in the audience for years. Damn. So I get up there, figure out the key I'm gonna sing in, and we start. The first song was a real old thirties or forties tune, "Five Foot Two." It's not exactly hard rock, but it does have a good swing to it. The next one, "Sinner Man," is in a minor key with a real fast beat. Gary and Nilan thought it was okay and the audience enjoyed it—at least they never threw any fruit up on stage.

That started a lasting friendship which continues to this day. Since that time, I've been on stage with them hundreds of times in Vancouver, Burnaby and North Van night spots. We have also been through many traumatic off-stage experiences—like fixing the brakes on Gary's ancient Valiant stranded up at Britannia Beach, and deep-sea diving—from my canoe—for my wallet in Deep Cove.

That first time I saw Gary on stage, he was playing the electric bass, the fiddle, and the mouth organ. I have since discovered he also plays the guitar and the mandolin, writes excellent music and has a good singing voice. He does all kinds of music from Dylan to western to rock, but the fiddle is his favourite instrument. I don't know anyone who plays a faster or better fiddle on the west coast.

Canada Geese—and Candidly Royal

My old buddy Al wanted to shoot one, possibly two, of the above. The latter, Candidly Royal, is Al's horse (other horse trainers say it's a dog, but Al says, "I know it's a dog, but it looks and eats like a horse"). The former are part of an annual hunting mission Al goes on.

Every fall, Al considers it a duty of sorts to send large numbers of Canadas to that great flyway in heaven. It's not that he's mean, it's just that he don't like to see too many honkers die of old age. You know, he doesn't want them to get crippled up with arthritis or Alzheimer's, and start flyin' backwards or end up in one of them old-geese homes where they get treated so poorly. He's a humanitarian hunter.

No, Al's not mean. But he is sneaky. Unlike some hunters, Al wouldn't dream of tackling a flock of Canadas with just a Browning twelve-gauge pump gun and a flack jacket. Nosirree, that would be too damn dangerous. A prudent hunter needs an edge, the kind you get with decoys and blinds.

Now Al was heading out on his annual prairie duck-hunting trip and he didn't have any decoys. His last ones all got shot or flew away or whatever. He had asked an old friend if he might borrow his decoys, but the guy said, "You can borrow my wife or my horse, but not my dog or my decoys."

But Al didn't give up. "No respectable hunter travels without decoys," he said. So the hunt was on for the elusive decoy. The best deal Al could find was at a sporting goods store down in Bellingham, Washington. Al volunteered me to drive him down and said we would leave on Tuesday morning. I must have a touch of Alzheimer's myself as I don't recall volunteering. But what could I do? No decoys, no dead geese. I'm a humanitarian too.

Tuesday morning arrives and Al, Ron, another friend and myself head for the border. Out of the blue, Al announces, "We have to make Cloverdale before eleven, and it's now ten thirty-eight." Why? I asked. "My horse is running to qualify in time trials at eleven."

Candidly Royal is the horse he and a partner are saving from the fox farm. Like I say, Al's a real humanitarian. He had to be to buy a three-legged horse for nine thousand dollars. But what the hell is money to a west coast fisherman?

We get there before the trial, and Al says to the horse, "When you get on the track, be sure to turn left. Then all you have to do is go with the flow." The horse got the left part okay, but he didn't flow too good. I think he needed a little higher octane fuel, or maybe new batteries. That was probably part of the problem—oh yes, four legs could have had a positive bearing on the outcome, too. Anyway, the horse didn't qualify but he did get home before dark, and we headed for the Blaine border crossing.

It was one in the afternoon on a weekday and we thought we should breeze through the border in three, maybe four minutes. Little did we know that at midnight the previous day the US Congress had frozen all monies to customs, so they were working with a skeleton staff. The bloody lineup was four miles long. It looked as though Candidly Royal might get home before we would.

So there we were: no food, no booze, no nothing. I'm

swearing at Al and the US Congress; Al is swearing at his horse; Ron is swearing at both of us for not leaving at five; we are all swearing to everything that's holy, and a couple things that ain't so holy; we are swearing especially never to cross that bloody border again, at least till the Chrysler needs gas.

After two hours in line, we finally get up to the little booth. The guy asks, "Where do you live?", "Y'all Canadian citizens?", "Where are you going, and for how long?", if we preferred the missionary position, and stuff like that. Al said he'd like to have a position like a missionary and Ron said, "What's a missionary?" I was too tired to explain.

Out on the freeway I drove real careful. Lots of good ol' Yankee boys down there pack guns, and they shoot people for not burnin' rubber when the light turns green. If they do shoot, all they get charged with is violating your civil rights. I didn't want anybody messin' with my civil rights.

We finally arrived at this huge sporting goods and gun store. They had more guns in that one store than the whole Canadian army—from machine guns and anti-tank weapons to muzzle loaders. It was Rambo heaven. Al had written two clerks' names on a piece of gasket and asked for the first name on his list. The chap across the showcase said, "He's on holidays." Oh-oh. Al asked for the other name. "He left for the day." Al explained he'd ordered some decoys three weeks before and that one of these guys had phoned and told him they were in. The clerk mumbled, "I'll see if I can find them."

Twenty minutes later the clerk returned. "I can't locate anything," he snarled, "maybe you guys can come back after the weekend."

"Weekend?" says Al. "Hell, I got to catch a plane tomorrow morning." The clerk gets a brain wave. "I'll try the warehouse next door." He disappeared for another twenty minutes. I had just explained to Al how the French half-breed hunters back home used to hunt geese without those damn decoys or any of that high tech stuff when the clerk returned. "I found them," he said. "You can drive your truck around back."

Al and I didn't like the sound of the word "truck" as we had come down there in my old Chrysler. Al was about to slash both his wrists when the clerk said, "Oh, one more thing. There's $120 air freight charges on them decoys."

Al exploded. "A hundred and twenty dollars? I was quoted twenty dollars freight over the phone!" He would have commited murder, but it was the guys behind the counter who had the guns. I could see the headlines in the Seattle papers: "Crazed Canadian Goose Hunters Slain in Dispute Over Decoys."

While Al was trying to figure how to make it back to Canada without taking out a second mortgage on his house or his first-born, I sauntered to the rear portion of the gun display. A kindly old grandfather-type clerk told me that they, the Americans, should "nuke" a certain Middle East country that was currently in the news. I would have explained that would be downright unneighbourly, but hell, he was over sixty-five and he was in the process of placing a machine gun on display. Besides, he had that kindly smile that said, "Man, I sure would like to see how this baby works," so I figured discretion was the better part of valour.

Al eventually out-manoeuvred the clerk on that extra freight charge and paid the bill. I drove my Chrysler around the back. It was all too apparent why that chap used the phrase, "drive your truck around back." Those decoys were in four huge boxes that would have filled a moving van. The only way we could get them to fit was by unpacking each and every one and stuffing them into the trunk.

"Al," I said as we drove off, "I hope this doesn't sour our relationship, but would you mind if I didn't 'volunteer' for the next hunting season?"

"To tell you the truth . . ."

"Don't bother," I said.

Other than Al getting mugged for another sixty dollars duty at the border, the rest of the trip was uneventful and we arrived back in Vancouver at eleven p.m. Al also had to buy three goalie pad bags to carry those birds on the plane, for which the airline dinged him for extra baggage. The way I figured it, any geese they got would be worth close on to four hundred dollars a pound.

In the end, Al got back from his great goose hunt and, other than a little redness in the eyes and a limp to starboard from twisting his ankle in a badger hole, he fared better than the geese. The official casualty list was, Canadas: 20, Mr. Brown: 0.

But don't go away. There's more. Their return flight from Grand Prairie was for Sunday morning, so a rancher drove them forty miles to the airport. Now, airports in some of those small northern towns are often not all that busy, but this one looked like it expired during the night. Nobody, just nobody, was around. Not even a gopher greeted this crew.

"Brown, are you sure you got the right day?" his partner, Eddy, asked. It's not unknown for hunters to lose a day or two up in those parts, sometimes even a week.

"Damn it's cold," said Al. "Eddie, did you bring anything along for snakebite?"

"Ya, but I ain't unpackin' it now. What does your ticket say?" Al couldn't read without his glasses so he handed the tickets to Eddie.

"Guess what?" said Eddie. "Our plane left yesterday. That's why there's cows walkin' on the runway. You dumb shit, we're stranded, and you owe me four hundred bucks."

Generally, when the stress level exceeds Mach 2, Al says, "Let's go for coffee. We need something for our nerves." But this time he said, "Let's take a little of that snake serum, drive back to the ranch and plan our attack." Forty ounces and forty miles later, they were back at the ranch, the decoys—minus removable heads— nesting quietly in the back of the truck. Looks like the price of them geese should be on the stock market like pork bellies.

Now Eddie had a job at the racetrack in Vancouver as a sort of horse judge, so he had to get back. So Al phoned the airline's head office in Vancouver and gave them a rough sketch of the problem. Head office said, "Tough beans. You miss your flight, you pay full price for the next one."

Time for the mortars and heavy artillery. Al figured if some wordsmith could say "a rose is a rose is a rose," he could say "a judge is a judge is a judge." He called the head honcho of that whole damn airline and announced that he was "Mr. Alan Brown, executive assistant to Judge Stewart . . ." (Al was shop steward in the fishermen's union at one time, so I suppose that could make one an executive of sorts.) "I booked a flight for the judge and myself from Vancouver, and the clerk must have written down the wrong return. As a result, we missed our flight, and the judge has to get back to a case in Vancouver."

Well, he wasn't lyin', but he was kinda fudgin' the truth. Eddie was a judge, and there was a "case" back in Vancouver (of Molson's or Labatt's). Eddie was a racehorse judge, and, like Al said, a judge is a judge. Why trouble this chap with details? The man on the phone said he would call back.

Two hours later the phone rang. It was from the Vancouver Airport and they want to speak to Judge Stewart. "Your Honour, we are sorry about the misunderstanding. Can we put you and your executive, Mr. Brown, on the ten o'clock Monday flight to Vancouver? There will be no charge of course, if that's agreeable to you."

Judge Stewart and his executive assistant, Mr. Brown, decided the arrangements would be just fine. Being gentlemen, they also accepted the apology.

Betty's Birthday Bash

My sister Betty had a birthday recently. Now ladies never reveal their age, and my sister keeps telling me she is a lady, so I'll leave her exact age a mystery. But there is one thing I can reveal—she is past the age of majority, leastwise chronologically.

Anyway, my two older sisters, Eileen and Jenny, conspired to throw a little birthday lunch for Betty at the Surrey Inn, a very nice hotel off the King George Highway in Surrey, some twenty-odd miles from Vancouver. Because Eileen lives on Vancouver Island, the plan was to pick her up at the Horseshoe Bay ferry terminal, drive to Lynmour, where Jenny lives, and then the three of us were to proceed to the hotel and meet Betty at noon. As it happened (this is going to sound like the plot from an old movie), my younger brother John was just a couple of blocks from the hotel at the time, laid up in Surrey Memorial Hospital, pretending he'd had a heart attack. Our plan included a visit to him after the meal.

We got to the Inn at twelve on the dot. We sat down, ordered coffee and waited. Then we had some more coffee and waited some more. Then more coffee and more waiting. Have you ever had that nagging little feeling like something ain't quite right? Well, we had it.

Now I'm no rocket scientist, but when you're supposed to meet somebody at twelve and it's five to one, it's time to get a little antsy. But I'm always diplomatic, and at such times, also optimistic. I thought, maybe that dumb shit got lost. Even guys who ain't rocket scientists need some nourishment, so I said, "I don't know about you turkeys, but I'm gonna eat, birthday or not."

So we had lunch (and it was damn good too). Afterwards I suggested to my sisters that seeing as how Betty never arrived, and seeing as I drove them out there, and seeing as they didn't have to buy Betty's lunch with the money they saved, they could buy my lunch. Well what do ya know, they went for it! It may have been an act of love, but more likely they were afraid of the long walk back to Vancouver. Either way, I got a free lunch.

By one forty-five, there was still no sign of the birthday girl, so we decided to leave. At the car, Eileen had a brainwave and decided to have another look at the address of the Surrey Inn, which she had written down. You guessed it. We were at the wrong place. No wonder that "dumb shit" couldn't find us.

I spent the next few minutes making sure Jenny didn't kill Eileen—I wanted that job myself. We burned off down the road and there, in the front parking lot of a run-down old place, was Betty. She was sitting in her car, a piece of dried-up fried chicken in one hand, a Styrofoam cup of coffee in the other, smiling. Damn, she is one hell of an actor. Maybe it's the aluminum pots she uses to cook with, but no self-respecting human being can be that tolerant. She even laughed at the dumb birthday cards we gave her.

Later, both Betty and Eileen got lost inside the hospital, proving there is justice in the universe after all. As for my brother John, he has since fled the hospital. He said he may survive another heart attack, but the food, never.

Happy Birthday, Betty.

Mexican Train Wreck

I'm a firm believer in the theory that if trains stayed in the station, boats stayed at the dock and planes stayed on the tarmac, there would be far fewer accidents. So far, the boats and planes part is still theory, but about train wrecks, I happen to know what I'm talking about.

The affair started in Vancouver with my very first plane ride. I was sitting in one of those cigar-shaped 727s, putting claw marks in the underside of the armrests, wondering how in hell a thing that size was ever going to fly. I was right over the wing but I wished I was at the tail end, 'cause a fella told me once that planes seldom back into mountains.

We sat there for two, maybe three years waiting to take off. Some joker asked, "Where are the parachutes?" but I didn't figure it was such a dumb question. Then the jets started making a high-pitched whine and this lumbering piece of aluminum and spare parts started to move. Nobody ever told me these bloody things taxi around about twelve miles before liftoff. And another thing: I always thought runways were smooth.

That's it, I thought. I'll never step onto another plane unless it has one of them strings running down the sides, like all the trains have. It's not the fear of flying that really bothers me, it's the crashing part I wouldn't enjoy. That, and the gnawing feeling that my old Chrysler back home has a good eight to ten thousand miles in her that I wouldn't be able to run off.

Looking out the window, I said to my wife, "Those people look like ants down there."

"They are ants," she said. "We haven't taken off yet."

My misgivings weren't helped by the fact that the pilot looked young enough to be playing with Tinkertoys.

Eventually my wife said, "You can come out from under the seat now, we're off the ground." Then I started wondering when that damn thing was going to level off. I didn't know planes flew up with the satellites. The seat belt light finally turned off and the flight attendants started pouring wine that tasted like old loggers' socks. My friend Dave got up and disappeared into the cockpit. For a minute I thought we might get a free ride to Cuba, but soon he came back with one of them first-time flyer certificates, signed by the captain, no less. It was reassuring to know our captain was old enough to sign his own name, though I noticed his crayons needed sharpening.

We were on our way to Guadalajara, Mexico. First, we had to make a stop in Smoke City, Los Angeles. The trick, or tricks, of landing in LA are 1) seeing the runway and 2) setting the plane down without pushing too many cars off the freeway. I didn't see my whole life flash before me but I did see a lot of licence plate numbers on the cars and trucks below, that's how close we were to the highway.

We got into the LA airport and I thought, my gawd! There's been a Mexican invasion. Then I realized that somebody has to mind the store while all the Californians are up in Canada chasing moose. The only thing that saved us in the airport bar was that I knew the Mexican word for beer. (A man always has to have priorities in the proper perspective.)

We took off again like a soggy sea gull. If it wasn't for those damn Wright brothers, we would have been travelling in a dome car, at a decent speed, enjoying the scenery.

Now anybody that thinks LA is smokey should try Guadalajara. What a soup! At least when you cut through the smog in Guadalajara you find a beautiful city—provided, of course, that you survive the cab ride from the airport. Anyone who thinks that bullfighting is dangerous hasn't ridden in a Mexican cab or bus. Why in hell they bother with traffic lights down there beats me. Maybe all them cab drivers are colour-blind. The only things that worked in our cab were the horn, and the picture of Jesus hanging from the rearview mirror. I'm not a religious man but I was beginning to find a strange comfort in that saying, "There are no foxhole atheists." Every contraption that moves down there (and some that don't) is festooned with Jesus, the Virgin Mary or Saint Christopher, and for damn good reason.

We stayed in Guadalajara a couple of days, checking out the old cathedrals, murals, flowers and all that good stuff. It is a truly magnificent old city. The Mexican people are for the most part poor, but nearly all the women were dressed in the latest fashion and they all seemed family-oriented. All in all, an extremely handsome people. Unlike North Americans, very few were overweight, so maybe poverty does have some plusses.

Everybody was hustling something, trying to make a few pesos, and there were lots of blind and crippled people begging on the street. The spirit of capitalism was alive and very, very well down there.

Our ultimate destination—a small seaport and fishing town called Manzanillo, where a friend of ours had a small house right on the beach—was still a couple of hundred miles away. We decided to make the journey in a first class bus. (In Mexico, that's the bus with the motor and wheels.)

Now, Guadalajara sits at quite a high elevation. The fact that sooner or later we had to go down some mountains to sea level in this old bus made me think we were going to need all them statues and icons up by the driver one more time. Sure enough, the driver went barrelling down that narrow road, completely oblivious to all chickens, goats, donkey carts and pedestrians who had the temerity to be using it. He only used one speed: flat out. Intersections, blind corners, stop signs be damned.

We were sitting right over the rear wheels when something started rapping under our feet. Having had some experience with truck tires, I knew one of them rear tire recaps was starting to fly apart. We were still going hell for leather, and that sound was getting louder and louder. So Dave made his way up front and explained in mostly sign language that one of the rear tires was falling apart. The driver pulled over and his buddy, who collected the fare, got out with his little blackjack, gave all those tires a rap and climbed back in.

I figured this guy was gonna baby the bus along to the next town, where we could put on another wheel and carry on. At least that's how we did it back in Chilliwack. But I was soon reminded we weren't in Chilliwack. This guy, I swear, was now going faster than ever, and the rapping sounds were getting louder and louder, so loud I thought that damn tire was gonna blow. Have you ever heard a tire blow that's carrying a hundred pounds pressure? To make matters worse, we were now going down the mountain to the sea, and that flapping tire was on the cliffside where the guardrails were supposed to be.

All of a sudden there was one loud bang right under our feet. I knew the recap had finally torn off, and we were now running on the cords. I think these people take such chances because they are so damn religious and ready to go at a moment's notice, but what about us heathens? Believe it or not, we rode that sick tire right into the bus station in Manzanillo. The driver and his buddy parked and took off into the station without a backward glance.

So you might think our troubles were over. No. I discovered that the name of the motel, and the little village it was in, had disappeared from my wallet. The rest of the crew was gonna kill me. I pulled that wallet apart ten times, and still nothing. I did, however, remember that the name of the motel was "La Posada." That should help. No again. Apparently "posada" in Spanish simply means motel; there were a lot of motels in the area. Then

I remember one other word, "Briscos." So I say to all them eager cabdrivers, "La Posada, Los Briscos; La Posada, Los Briscos." Nothing but blank stares.

While I was considering self-immolation, Dave started looking through the phone book to see if anything looked familiar. We found out later this particular motel didn't even have a telephone. Just then another cab drove up.

"La Posada, Los Briscos, Senor?" I pleaded.

"Los briscos, si," said the cabby, "five hundred pesos." By then I would have given him five thousand, so we piled into the cab, and three miles down the road he pulled off to the beach. There, in lights, is the name "La Posada." Why anyone would name a motel "motel", beats me.

We paid the cabdriver and walked to the cabins. Pinned with a knife to one of the huge wooden doors was a note from our friend: "You'll find plenty of rum and tequila inside, help yourself. See you in a couple of days."

The place was fantastic. We were so close to the beach that the thunderous breakers rattled the widows. Bougainvillaea nearly covered the cabins. The beach was dotted with little straw lean-tos to fend off the hot sun. When we weren't in that warm water, we would ride an ancient Leyland bus with wooden floors into the little town of Manzanillo for dinner or to shop. Give me the smaller towns any day, it was just a great holiday.

The longer I stayed in Mexico, the more I realized that all the BS about Mexicans being lazy was just that, bullshit. They're a hard-working, friendly, industrious people, and as far as I can tell, their only sin is being poor.

After a week in Manzanillo it was time to head back to Guadalajara. This time we planned to take something safer than a bus. So we tried asking a policeman (who was wearing a pearl-handled revolver slung low in the fashion of a movie cowboy) where we could find the train station. He didn't understand what the hell we were talking about until we made noises like a train. Then he pointed down the street.

The difference between first class and second class on Mexican trains was about a buck, so we decided to splurge. The trip cost us about five bucks per ticket. Before leaving, Dave and I took the precaution of buying a big bottle of El Presidente rum in case we stepped on a scorpion or had some other such disaster.

The train pulled out a half-hour late, but down there nobody counts. We travelled past banana and coconut groves, and rumbled over little trestles under which women washed clothes in streams; we saw pigs tied by one front leg to a tree, and chickens and kids and skinny dogs in farmers' yards; we saw burros, and the odd horse. If one had to describe the whole scene in two words, it would be "picturesque poverty."

Riding along, I suggested to Dave that we had enough luggage to carry without packing around those full bottles of rum. He agreed. The women didn't think our getting hammered was such a great idea, but they didn't have to carry suitcases stuffed with five thousand pounds of trinkets for the kids back home. So there we sat, each with half a bottle, getting all philosophical and smart, solving the world's problems and thinking about quitting our jobs back home.

It was about three in the afternoon, and hotter than hell because even first class didn't include anything as exotic as air-conditioning. Dave had just gone to the can at the front of the car and was making his way back when he started wobbling back and forth like crazy. I thought, "Holy cow, that rum must be strong." The swaying got worse and worse, and the cars up ahead were whipping back and forth like a sidewinder.

"Holy Christ," I said, "we're off the rails." Just then the cars started tipping over. Talk about a rough ride! When the train finally came to a halt, our car was at about a thirty-degree angle. The cars up ahead were far worse and looked as though they would topple at any minute. We sobered up in a hurry, grabbed our stuff and scrambled off the train.

We walked up to the forward cars and helped a lot of the elderly Mexican women off who were crying and panic-stricken.

Other than a few bruises, though, no one was badly hurt. A bunch of army types who had been on the train just disappeared down the track in the direction we had come, not giving a damn about the other passengers.

The steel rail under those cars looked like a bunch of spaghetti. The locomotive's batteries were torn apart. It was obvious that our train wasn't going anywhere for a few days, so we asked a man where we might catch a bus. He pointed across a cane field, where we could see what looked like a highway in the distance. I did notice, however, that most everyone else headed back along the tracks in the direction those chivalrous army types had taken.

We started out across this stubbly, fresh-cut cane field. It was a good thing we'd drunk that rum, since it was scorching hot and we were walking with luggage in six inches of burning sand. I thought we'd die right there in the desert. There was no shade anywhere, and that sun bounced off the sand like the outskirts of hell.

Finally, we got to where the road was supposed to be. It was just an old wagon trail. About six or eight miles down this dirt track we could see a couple of church steeples, so we decided to plod in that direction.

"Whose idea was this damn train ride, anyway?" complained the women. They should have been carrying those steamer trunks.

Behind us we saw dust rising, and in a minute or two an ancient, beat-up pickup truck pulled up. It was jammed with cane cutters carrying huge machetes. None of the workers spoke any English, but they saw the train on its side in the distance and figured what had happened. Although the old truck was loaded with sun-blackened, sweaty workers, we managed to squeeze the luggage and the two women on board. When the truck pulled away those women looked as though they'd never be seen alive again. I wish to hell I had had a camera handy to record the look of terror on their faces. (And for recording the look of relief on our faces at getting rid of that damned luggage.)

Dave and I started hoofing it toward the church steeples. Those Spaniards sure did leave some good landmarks around, though I doubt that crossed their minds when they built them. Our luck was changing fast, 'cause coming up behind us was a two-wheeled cartload of hay pulled by a tiny burro and a skinny white horse. The farmer stopped and motioned for us to climb up on the load. He didn't have to ask us twice. We clambered up onto that sweet-smelling green hay. What a relief! The farmer spoke no English at all, but we managed to communicate a few things, and I noticed that the harness he had on those animals was made out of old automobile tires. We could certainly take some lessons from those people in ingenuity and resourcefulness.

The farmer let us off in a little town whose name I can't recall. We gave him a handsome tip, probably a couple days wages to him, but what the hell when you've just come through a train wreck. We eventually found our wives, Midge and Yvonne, at the bus station.

Dave said, in his sympathetic way, "If you guys had been murdered, I wonder what would have happened to my expensive camera?"

"Maybe you could have claimed it on your homeowner's policy," I said.

There didn't seem to be anybody to reimburse us for that half train-ride, but like I said, the whole thing cost less than five dollars each. Where else could you have as much fun for five bucks?

We caught the next bus to Guadalajara and arrived home without any more earth-shattering events—that is, if you don't count me going into cardiac arrest on the return plane ride.

Brown Beats BC Hydro?

At the risk of getting shot, I'm gonna share another Al Brown escapade with you.

Al had an old combination troller/gillnetter that served him well through the years, but like all equipment—and especially old wooden boats—it needed a little fixin' from time to time. Actually, the *Sea Deuce* needed more than a little fixin', it required major surgery. If it was a patient, the nurse would have said, "Condition grave, no visitors."

Al has a few strange habits and the main one is, he doesn't like to throw anything away, including old fish boats. So he hauls this relic into his backyard where he planned to work a few miracles. Then he built a frame shed sheeted with plywood and plastic around the old *Sea Deuce* to keep out of the wind and the rain. It was still damn cold in there, however, so he strung an extension cord from the house and installed a couple of small electric heaters.

Well, one problem seems to generally lead to another, maybe even two or three. The trouble with the heaters was that they didn't throw enough heat to dry the old tub out, which was one of the original purposes of the whole operation. The other problem was that Al was going to have to get a second mortgage on his house just to pay for the increased Hydro bill.

One thing about Al, he generally ain't stuck for long, and when it comes to savin' money, especially his, he gets as inventive as Ben Franklin or Thomas Edison. One cold morning as Al was walking out to the boatshed, he noticed that the tree beside the shed was mighty close to the power line coming to his house. You guessed it: he went up that tree, bared each of the incoming wires, and ran two lines down the tree into his boatshed. That little operation had two distinct advantages. One, he could now put in enough heaters to dry out the boat, and two, the price was right.

Al worked in shirt-sleeve comfort on his old boat for the next few months and kept telling me how damn smart he was. I told him I never could figure if he was real smart or just real cheap.

Now, we all know what Burns said about the best-laid plans. How was Al to know his neighbour would have line trouble, and that while the keen-eyed lineman was up that pole he'd see a bandit power line running down a tree?

Al was mowing his lawn when the Hydro man walked up and said, "Do you live here?"

"Yeah," he said, "what can I do for ya?"

"There's a power line running down that tree," said the Hydro fellow. "I'll have to climb up there and take it down."

Al acted surprised as hell about the line, but the lineman didn't really believe him. Al figured the best defence was a good offence, so he told that chap, "You're on private property and you ain't going up my tree." His figuring was that the guy would take off and give him time to get the line down.

Well, the Hydro guy had a little artillery of his own. He simply walked back to the lane, climbed another pole and disconnected the power to Al's property. Then he got in his truck and drove away. These guys play pretty rough, thought Al, but no problem. He just went up the tree, took down the line, hid the evidence and phoned BC Hydro to get reconnected.

With all that free power he'd had, he still could pay the reconnection cost and be way ahead of the game.

"Certainly, Mr. Brown," said a pleasant-sounding man. "But first we will have to come out and do an inspection. Purely routine Hydro policy, you understand."

Al said, "Okay," then he started thinking. "What the hell does he mean, routine policy, inspection and stuff? Isn't it all computed on the square root of a turkey's ass or the gizzard of a chicken on the ides of March?" A couple of hours later a Hydro truck drove up and a man in white coveralls with a clipboard and a curled-up waxed moustache stepped out.

"Mr. Brown, this will only take a few minutes, just Hydro policy before we reconnect power."

Al didn't like the look of that waxed moustache, sort of like the kind you see on dogcatchers and bylaw enforcement officers.

Ten minutes later the moustache emerged from the basement with the verdict.

"I'm sorry Mr. Brown, your house is condemned. We will be unable to give you Hydro until the house is totally rewired. Your 30-amp service is totally inadequate."

"Condemned," Al explodes, "what the hell do you mean condemned?"

"Simply that," said the moustache, "your 30-amp service is totally inadequate. The wiring is all shot and improperly installed. It's a wonder the place hasn't burned down years ago."

Then the moustache tacked a blue paper on the front door stating the house was unsafe, warned him it was an offence to remove the paper, wished him a good day and drove off. Al told me later, "Those bastards really play hardball."

Three weeks and damn near a divorce later, Al's house had been completely rewired with a 220-amp service. So he phoned Hydro to come and hook him up. They arrived, hooked up his power and left. Al figured it was all over and done with. His wife turned on the stove later that day and it only got a tiny bit warm. So my friend went outside to see what the problem was and found out the linemen had hooked him up as though he still had 30-amp service.

Back to the telephone. This time Al asked the supervisor how long those turkeys had been playing with electricity, whether his linemen could walk down the street and chew gum at the same time and lots of nasty stuff like that.

Now this approach wasn't getting him any brownie points down at Hydro, but at least he was getting a little satisfaction and revenge for all that wiring they made him do.

"Mr. Brown," said the man from Hydro. "we've had a fair amount of problems with this account, so here's what I am going to do. The line crews have all left for the day, so I will have to call two men back, and that will be four hours each at double time plus sixty dollars service, flat rate. So if your line is not hooked up wrong as you say it is, you will be billed for the total amount, which comes to $364."

"Good," said Al, "just don't send those two amateurs that were out here last time."

Soon the Hydro crew arrived and, sure enough, they agreed the other fellows had screwed up. Ten minutes later everything in the house was working and there was peace in the valley.

One day I said to Al, "Al, how much money did you save on that Hydro scam?"

"Go to hell, you smart bastard," was all he said.

Now, what do you think of a friend like that?

Wanna Buy a Duck?

All mother-in-law jokes aside, the general consensus seems to be that your average mother-in-law is a fairly difficult person to love. But the woman I'm talkin' about, my ex-mother-in-law, wasn't average, so loving her was easy as pie.

Now Bea told me the other day that if I identify her in this story, not only will I be her ex-son-in-law, I will be her late ex-son-in-law. So suffice it to say Bea was the nursing supervisor in the old North Van General Hospital for twenty-five years, and that I respect her very much.

When Bea retired from nursing, she and her husband Jim bought a condo on Martin Street in White Rock. White Rock at that time still had a few breathing spaces—hell, you could even see the water in spots.

One day Bea mentioned to Jim that she would like to cook a duck for their next Sunday dinner and asked if he would pick one up at Safeway. Half an hour later, Jim returned with a frozen duck and put it in the freezer. Then things got a little complicated. Doris, a friend of Bea's who lived in the apartment next door, was moving out. She told Bea she had some frozen stuff she didn't want and asked if Bea wanted it. Bea said, "Sure," and Doris put the goods in Bea's freezer.

Next Sunday came around and Bea went to get the duck from the freezer. "I thought you bought a duck," she said, looking at the package. "This is a chicken."

Jim said, "I asked for a duck, and that damn clerk sold me a chicken." Fuming mad, he set off for Safeway with the bird of contention under his arm. As soon as he got to the store, he started giving some poor clerk holy hell. The manager heard all the ruckus and came over to see what was causing the problem. "Does this look like a duck to you?" snapped Jim, holding out the poor old chicken.

"Nope, that's definitely not a duck," said the manager. "What's more, that's a SuperValu sticker on it. I don't believe it came from our store."

"Now you look here young man, I might be old but I ain't that senile yet," replied Jim, who is nearly stone deaf. "I asked for a duck and I don't give a damn what kind of sticker is on it. I bought it at this store and I ain't leavin' here till I get my duck."

"Well that's the strangest thing I ever heard of," said the manager. "Tell you what I'll do. I will give you another duck, no charge."

"What about the chicken?" asked Jim.

"You can keep the chicken too."

That Sunday, Bea and Jim had a fine duck dinner. (In retrospect, I wonder why in hell we weren't invited. I'll have to talk to Bea about that.)

A month later, Bea decided to clean out her freezer. What did she find buried in back of the freezer? Yep, a nice big plump frozen duck. It seemed Jim really had bought a duck after all; it got pushed right to the back of the freezer when Dora was putting the other stuff in.

Did you ever want to kill somebody but didn't know who? That was Bea's dilemma. Suicide was maybe a little closer to Bea's thoughts, as she was so damn embarrassed about the whole situation. People of her generation are, for the most part, deadly honest, and Bea was certainly no exception.

So she marched right down to that Safeway store, asked for the manager and told him of the mistake. She said she'd pay for the lost duck right there. Well, the manager just about killed himself laughing. He told Bea he would't take a penny for the bird and that he had insurance for that kind of thing. In fact, he insisted she take the duck home. "Enjoy your dinner." (Now that I mention it, we weren't invited to *that* duck dinner either!)

So there you go, Bea. Nobody knows who you are. In fact, I'm safe mentioning that your last name starts with the letter F, and your nickname is the same as that John—you know, that Montreal Canadiens bad guy who used to get into all those fights.

Oh, Bea? One more thing. I really don't mind missing the odd duck dinner. Matter of fact, I don't like duck, especially the ones that look like chicken.

The Brick

Go ahead, shoot me. I've got one last tale about Alan S. Brown. "He's not sound," is an expression Al always uses to explain any unusual behavior or to identify those of his numerous friends, mostly fishermen, whose cables are a little stretched. It's true, Al's friends are not rocket scientists or brain surgeons. But before jumping on them, let me tell you that Al has pulled some strange manoeuvres himself. Take, for instance, the one with the brick.

Now you might expect a man who has made fishing his life for the past forty years, and who has renewed his commercial licence each and every one of those years, to have stamped on his brain the annual date by which he has to renew that licence. You'd probably even expect it of an old gillnetter with half his brains beaten out. After all, his livelihood depends on it. But can Al remember that date? No way.

A couple of years ago, Al (up to his usual speed) forgets to renew his herring fishing licence by the deadline, which happened to fall on Good Friday and Friday the thirteenth. An average guy would certainly remember a date like that, but the thing here is, we ain't dealing with your average guy. If you won't take my word for it, just ask Al's wife.

So Al panics and phones the fisheries office. All he gets is a taped message: "We are not available till 9:00 a.m. Monday. If you wish to leave a message, etc., etc." Now that licence, if he loses it, is worth anywhere from fifty to a hundred thousand dollars, and that's not counting the medical bills he's gonna need when his wife Norah gets through with him.

But Mr. Brown is ingenious, like that Leonardo character that was cooking things up a few centuries ago. He finds a nice heavy brick and wraps his cheque around it. Included is a note saying, "I'm Al Brown. I came here to renew my licence before the deadline, but the place was closed a minute early. I'll pay for the plate glass window this brick came through." He figures paying for a new window is peanuts if it saves his licence.

The only hitch Al can see in his plan is that some passerby might report him for vandalism. And that could be solved, he decides, by calling a beat cop ahead of time and telling him he would pay for the damage, blah, blah. (I told you Mr. Brown may not be running on all cylinders.)

Al ponders over that plan for an hour or so and realizes a little modification may be in order. What if the cop doesn't think the idea is all that hot? (On rare occasions, even old gillnetters can see flaws in the great scheme of things, provided, of course, they ain't layin' under a barstool some place). So Al scraps Plan A, including the part about the cop, and heads down to the Department of Fisheries offices at two in the morning.

Now the old Peter Principle starts workin'. The window that Al needs to throw that brick through is on the fourth floor. Al is a lot of things, but he sure the hell ain't no four-storey brick man. Come to think of it, I don't know who is. Those slingshots he and I made that summer could have reached the fourth floor, but not with a brick payload. He could almost see his licence, and consequently his life, sinking like his old gillnetter the *Sea Deuce* down at False Creek.

But when push comes to shove and the water gets a little

rough, Al just throttles back and takes stock. He walks around to the front of that building, like his three-year-old grandson would have done in the first place, and guess what he sees? A huge sign pasted to the front door saying that due to the Good Friday holiday, the Fisheries Department was extending the closing licence date to the following Monday.

Next morning he has the nerve to tell me how damn smart he was!

It's a year later now, and guess what? He forgot the deadline for his herring licence again. This time he ain't even lucky enough to have Friday the thirteenth helping him out.

Like I say, a man gets a lot of sun back in one of them old boats.

Windows in the Dark

My brother-in-law Jack, known as Fergie to most of us, is an X-ray technician in White Rock, BC. You wouldn't call him a wolf in sheep's clothing, but you could call him a farmer in X-ray technician's clothing.

Now, Fergie knows a lot about his profession. But what he knows about farming and building and all that stuff related to the pioneer life he loves so much, you could, well . . . put it this way, you could make a thumbnail sketch of everything he knows about that on your pinky.

But minor details like not knowing what he's doing have never bothered old Fergie. He has plenty of friends, and he has plenty of books. Fergie is a travelling encyclopedia salesman's idea of heaven on earth—they spot that big S on his head from miles. Whenever he runs into something he can't figure out, he buys another book. To this date, it doesn't seem to have helped a hell of a lot, but Fergie don't quit all that easy.

Fergie has friends coming out of the woodwork, and for good reason. He's a very gregarious, hospitable, fun-loving guy. He's also generous to a fault, a terrific host and one hell of a mean cook. Not only that, he's fairly bright, as long as he's kept away from the hammer and power tools.

Back in the late seventies Fergie's pioneer instincts took over and he prowled the Fraser Valley in search of land. Fergie believed in the Chinese philosophy regarding land. That is, that they aren't making any more of it and, in most ways, it's better than money.

He eventually found ten acres of bush on Sylvester Road, a few miles past Mission. The first time I saw the property it was covered in two feet of snow, and the snow was covered with all sorts of strange animal tracks. I was thinking, "I hope old Fergie don't plan to build out here in this remote wasteland, 'cause it looks far more suited to the fur trade than farming." But how can you kill a man's enthusiasm? I said it looked great, would make an ideal building site, should be fine for a big garden, and a whole lot of bullshit like that.

"We should be able to clear a couple acres and throw up a house in no time," said Fergie. I didn't like the sound of that word "we" all that much, but I didn't want to throw cold water on the idea. Secretly I was thinking a landslide or a flood might take the whole ten acres away before the deal was completed. After all, it was between two creeks, right at the base of a mountain.

No flood, no landslide, and soon the phone rang at home. It was Fergie. He was jumping off the ground; he had made the deal. Now he needed some fenceposts hauled out. I just happened to have a big truck, and there went the whole damn ballgame.

Nearly every weekend for the next couple of summers we fenced, cleared land and camped on the site. It was a great place for all the in-laws and out-laws and friends who would spend a day or two out in the good air and black night skies, away from the city. There was even a crystal clear creek nearby to swim in.

Fergie wanted to build a 20x30-foot house with a hip barn-style roof. We made all our own roof trusses, and I cut all the shakes from old cedar snags on the property. Fergie brought out a huge antique kitchen stove from Saskatchewan and had it all re-silvered. He also had a potbellied stove for extra heat.

Fergie would often cook for fifteen or twenty people on that antique range and nobody ever suffered from malnutrition. However, there was a price, or prices, to pay. You had to work and you had to listen to those damn hospital jokes. I still don't know which was the toughest.

It seems whenever you have a Garden of Eden, somebody is always getting into those damn apples. Out at Fergie's place, it wasn't apples, it was plastic. And it wasn't Eve in the garden, it was black bears. They liked to chew up the two-inch plastic water line that snaked down from the creek. Generally, the bears only mangled the pipe. The water pressure at the house used to drop, and we would walk along the pipeline until we found the sprinkler system, compliments of Mr. Bear. It seemed they couldn't resist putting their teeth through that black plastic.

One other, or rather, two other problems with that water supply were the drastic rise or fall of that mountain stream, and ice in the line in the wintertime. Old Fergie was beginning to find this pioneering life not as romantic as he had at first anticipated.

Not to worry. Fergie is the eternal optimist. Like I said before, could be his bubble is a little off-plumb. Another minor quirk Fergie harboured was a fanatical fascination with old stuff. Can't hit him too hard in that department. I'm one of the world's largest junk collectors myself. (Of course it could be that my cables are stretched, too.)

Anyway, when we built this house, Fergie insisted on using old wooden windows he had collected through the years. Now I have nothing against old wooden windows, but when you live in the bush in a rain forest, you need all the light you can get. Those little old-fashioned windows just didn't cut it.

After about six months of living in the dark and bumping over things, Fergie started to see the light—to use an inappropriate figure of speech. The house needed more light. Electric lights were a possibility, but Fergie, who has a little Scottish blood, decided it was too damn costly to keep the power company living like fat cats just so he could find the front door.

Now, just to reassure you folks who may have to go for X-rays from time to time, technicians, on the odd occasion, are capable of using fundamental logic. Especially if it is pointed out to them in a courteous, diplomatic fashion, such as I did one day. "Fergie, you dumb shit," I said. "Why don't you put in some bigger windows and let a little light in this Black Hole of Calcutta?"

"Good idea," he said. "Why don't we do that."

Me and my big mouth. Damn. I found a couple of huge plate glass windows at a used building supply and took them out to Fergie's in my truck. By the time I arrived, it was too late to go to work, so we stored the windows against a tree, out of the way of kids and dogs. Kids you can replace, but them big second-hand windows are hard to come by. Good dogs are hard to find nowadays, too.

One snowy winter night sometime later, Fergie phoned and said he was all by himself with a bottle of rum. He wasn't too sure it would keep till morning once he got the top off. I figured, what's a thirty-five-mile drive in a snowstorm when a man has that kind of trouble? When I arrived an hour later, it was snowing and drifting like hell. It was a good thing the rum was on that end of the journey, and not the other way around.

We were into that rum a few inches—or quite a few centimeters—when I said to Fergie, "What do you say we put in those big windows?"

He said, "You must be getting truck exhaust fumes inside the cab. It's too damn cold, it's snowing like hell and it's blacker than bear shit out there."

"Fergie," I said. "You disappoint me. I thought you were a pioneer, not a candy-assed wimp."

After a few more compliments and a couple more shots, we put one hell of a fire on in both stoves, and I took the flashlight and measured the windows. Then, with a level and a square, I drew out the opening to cut.

"Holy God," said Fergie, "that's half the bloody wall. We're gonna freeze to death." Without all that antifreeze, he may have been right.

Then I fired up the chain saw. Boy, there's nothing like the sound of a chain saw inside a house. There was lots of smoke 'cause Fergie used to really go heavy on the oil in the gas mixture. I hit a few nails, but what the hell; that old chain was in bad shape to start with. Five minutes later the wall fell out with a crash, and there we were, looking at a winter wonderland.

We slipped and slid out to get the big windows. What do you know? The glazing had come away in the weather and the heavy plate glass was ready to fall out of the frame as soon as we moved it. I could see the newspaper story, "Two Drunks Bleed to Death After Being Cut With Broken Glass . . . ambulance unable to affect a rescue due to deep snow and blizzard . . . mystery as to why they were working in such adverse conditions at that hour . . . only thing left alive was the cat, who was stiff with cold due to the fact half the building was missing."

It was too dangerous to move the windows frame and all, so we eased the plate glass out. Then it was a simple matter of setting the window casing in the hole in the wall. Later we put the plate in, sort of haywire-like. By then we were beat. That rum bottle was lookin' pretty damn anaemic, so we hit the sack.

Next morning Fergie got up to make bacon and eggs. "Holy Christ," he hollered, "I can see the whole damn mountain out there."

"Fergie," I said. "Would you mind keeping it down? I got a hangover."

Happiness

Passing time, seconds flying;
  Hours, days, years of trying.
Soon or later, green grass growing;
Nothing for this life we're showing.
Banker, beggar—all will pass,
Each will find his plot of grass.
Pillows damp in rooms of darkness,
Laugh the clowns throughout the day.

If I upon a judge's bench
Were asked what is success,
I'd not reply a long long life,
Just a minute's happiness.